LIFE
&
FAVOR

V.M. JACKSON

LIFE & FAVOR
Copyright © 2018 V.M.Jackson

Life & Favor is a work of fiction. The events and
characters that are described are imaginary and
are not intended to refer to specific places or living
persons.

Acknowledgements

Tariq Sr.,

They say if a writer loves you, you can never die. Would you agree? Our love has been described more vividly than one could ever imagine. The feelings we have for each other have lived and breathed. Because I was here, you will always exist. Your name is permanently etched into paper; your physical descriptions printed in ink. You will always be frozen in time.

Some of the moments we've spent together, good and bad, have been secretly coded, documented, reflected on, glorified, and transformed into poetry. I turned even the ugliest sides of us into something lovable, perfect. They say writers are obsessively observant, they feel the rawest form of emotions, they see human behavior as something to always take note of. And it's true; you were my favorite character.

I have authenticated you, stored you, and can recall certain scenes whenever I like. I have made our love thrive in words, sentences, paragraphs. Your texture, your sound, your scent; I bought it to life. You will be kept alive eternally and will forever remain my favorite, truest love story I have ever written.

A million hugs and kisses to my children, Tariq, Ava, and Judah, for giving me the opportunity to mother differently than my own mother did.

Chapter 1

I couldn't help but laugh as I sat in my grandmother Elaine's house eating chicken and watching home videos of my crazy family. I always went to church with her on Sunday mornings, and afterward we'd stop for Kentucky Fried Chicken while we anticipated the arrival of the SEPTA bus to take us back to her senior citizen home. Once we arrived at her apartment, we'd kick off our shoes, eat, and relax in front of the TV until my mother came to pick me up. This particular Sunday, my grandmother decided to put on some home videos of me when I was little. I sat in her living room laughing at the antics of my younger self until I cried real tears.

"I tell your mother all the time, you should've been a little boy," my grandmother giggled, "you run, jump, climb, and fall just like them."

In the video, I was five years old. It was Easter Sunday, and my mother had dressed me in a beautiful, white ruffled dress that flared out from my waist to my knees. The itchy petticoat underneath made my dress even fluffier. I wore matching white ruffled socks, white patent leather shoes, and white ruffled bows that held my long beautiful ponytails together. My mother was the queen of coordination and wouldn't have had it any other way.

My dark skin was as smooth as butter. I watched as a wide grin spread across my face, revealing the spaces where my two front teeth had fallen out. My mother stood a few feet away, watching while I danced along a bench outside our church. I walked back and forth like a gymnast on a balance beam, swinging my white pocketbook like a pair of nunchucks.

"Mystery, *please stop* swinging that pocketbook before you hit somebody in the face with it," she scolded.

"Yes ma'am," I obeyed.

"And get down from that bench before you—"

Before she could finish her sentence, I was already in mid-jump. I intended to do a front flip and land on my feet like Michelangelo from *Ninja Turtles*, but I looked more like brown paint from a painter's palette that fell off the brush and splattered onto the concrete. Time seemed to slow down as I fell. In the seconds it took for me to reach the ground, I knew it was going to hurt. I fell forward when I landed, and my pocketbook flew into the street. My beautiful white dress was now dirty, and worst of all, both of my knees had scraped the ground and were bleeding. My mother gasped, rushing to my aid with widened eyes.

"Mystery!" she hissed, grabbing me by the arm and scooping me up. "Are you okay?" She looked at my bloody knees and regretted asking.

"I think I broke my legs," I screamed deliriously in pain as tears ran down my face.

"They didn't break *this* time," she assured me, "but if you keep playing Russian roulette like that, you just might get your wish next time. You're such a fearless child," she placed me on my feet and shook her head. "No one in our family is as brave as you. Mystery was the *perfect* name for you."

Entranced by the video, I felt bad for my younger self.

"If that isn't the pot calling the kettle black," my grandmother shook her head. "You are your *mother's* child. She was *just* like you when she was little—wild, free, and fearless."

"She wasn't scared of anything?" I asked.

"No," my grandma laughed. "That fool would play in traffic if she could've." She paused. "Well, wait a minute, I take that back. She *was* scared of one thing. She was afraid of giving birth to you."

"Why?"

"She miscarried a couple years before you were born, so she spent her entire pregnancy with you in fear. She was also afraid to bring you into this world and fail. It didn't matter to her that she was *raised* by a good mother. She still doubted that she could *be* a good mother. Oh, but the day she went into labor, it was like time stood still." My grandmother got up with a smile, making her way to the VCR. "Take a look at this."

She popped in the video of my birth. It looked pretty gross, and as I sat there I made a mental note of it, and subconsciously scratched *childbirth* off my bucket list. I watched in utter disgust as the doctors took me out of my mother and cut the umbilical cord. I glanced over at my grandmother, watching along with the biggest smile on her face. As the doctors placed me in my mother's arms for the first time, I watched the trauma of childbirth disappear from her face, and her eyes light up like the stars.

She swaddled me in her arms, looked down at me, and my grandmother was right—it was as if time had stood still.

"Hi Mystery," my mother grinned and blushed so hard you could see all thirty-two of her teeth. "It's so nice to finally meet you. Look how *beautiful* you are."

As the video played, tears welled up in my eyes. Before I knew it, they had broken away and trickled down my face.

"Mystery? *Mystery*?" a sweet female voice summoned me out of my imagination. "Are you all right?"

I blinked rapidly, trying to force my mind back to reality. When I came to, I realized I was never at my grandmother's house, rather, I was sitting in an office in front of my therapist, Dr. Robinson.

"I'm sorry," I responded, my voice barely audible, "Where were we?"

"You were telling me the earliest memory you had of your mother." Reaching for a tissue, Dr. Robinson handed it to me to wipe my falling tears.

I'd been a patient of hers twice per week after school for over three years. Every time she'd ask me to tell her a story about my past, I'd get lost in my imagination, thinking about the way I *wished* the story went instead of facing the cold, bitter truth of what really happened. Today was another reality check. Dr. Robinson was a nice woman. She was friendly with an overall pleasant personality and tidy appearance, but her office always gave me the creeps. The walls were bare, painted with an uninviting cream color. Her décor and furniture dated back to the early seventies, and today might get rejected as a donation by the Salvation Army. The carpet was dark brown and probably pre-dated the Stone Age. To be fair, she had a really beautiful Tibetan singing bowl on the floor that I always wanted to play with. There was a tacky looking plastic water feature on each of the end tables beside the couch, and an inspirational quote on the wall- curled at the corners, almost ready to fall apart. In fact, everything in her office was flimsy and looked like it was ready to fall apart. Not a good sign for someone who was supposed to help you reconstruct your life, but she was the only person around these days that seemed to care. My insurance paid for her undivided attention, and at this season of my life, attention from *somebody* was much needed.

"Do you want to finish telling me what you saw in your grandmother's home videos?" she asked sweetly.

Gathering my thoughts, I took a deep breath and cleared my throat.

"The video of my birth cut off shortly after the doctors handed me to my mother. She was embarrassed and disappointed because she thought I'd turn out light-skinned like her. She had an obsession with fair skinned babies, and she was certain I would come out golden brown with a full head of hair. Instead, I came out chocolate and bald. She *hated* dark skin, and she hated me. Of all the synonyms she could've used to describe my breathtaking complexion, she described me as being the color of dirt. The thought of her having a dirty-looking baby made her sick to her stomach. I'm sure of it, because every time she looked at me, she looked like she wanted to throw up

More tears formed in my eyes, but I quickly wiped them away before they fell.

"The video of me on Easter Sunday ended after she told me to get down from the park bench, and I didn't listen. She got so mad, she yanked me off the bench and knocked me right into the concrete. *Broke both of my legs.* My grandmother cut the camera off immediately and ran to my rescue.

Dr. Robinson shook her head.

"Do you ever wish things were different between you and your mother?" Dr. Robinson asked.

"Always," I said softly. "I was about five or six when I realized she didn't love me. Of course, the way in which I knew it, was different from how I would understand it now. Still, I knew."

Dr. Robinson nodded. "How old are you, Mystery?"

"I'm fifteen."

"You're a very intelligent young lady for fifteen," She smiled, removing her black-framed prescription glasses. "How about we end here. We can continue this conversation during our next visit."

"Sure," I nodded, getting up from the chair.

I wasn't in the mood to talk about it anymore, anyway.

Grabbing my schoolbag, I waved goodbye to Dr. Robinson and proceeded out the door, glancing at my wristwatch on the way out. It was just after five pm, and I was in no rush to get home. I lived with my Aunt Carol, or as I called her in my diary, *Cruella Deville*. I knew the second I stepped into the house, she would start with her drama. Instead of walking to the bus stop, I headed down the street to the public library, where I could read and do my homework in peace.

Chapter 2

Cruella De-Ville

I sat in the library for thirty minutes awaiting my turn to use the computers. When one did open up, I walked over to it and sat down. Before my fingers could even touch the keyboard, my cellphone went off. I reached down to get it and saw that it was Aunt Carol calling.

Here we go. I braced myself.

"Hello?" I answered hesitantly, the hair on the back of my neck standing up in anticipation of the sound of her voice.

"*Where* are you!?" she fussed. Her booming voice blared through the phone into the ears of some of the people sitting at the computers next to me. They glanced in my direction at her yelling.

"I'm in the library," I whispered. "I came here after my appointment because I didn't feel like getting on the bus yet."

"Did you call me or Steve to let one of us know what you didn't *feel* like doing?"

"No, I—"

"My children can't stay at the house by themselves. They need an older person there with them. The neighbor just called me threatening to call the police because Michael, James, *and* Jacob are all outside riding their bikes in the street unsupervised."

8

Then go home and supervise them, I thought sarcastically. "I'm sorry," I responded. "I—"

"So, my children are left unattended and are *now* in danger because your fat ass decided you wanted to be grown and didn't *feel* like going home after counseling."

Her insults felt like a sharp dagger stabbing into my chest. She called me so many names on a consistent basis, you'd think I would be used to it. *Some things I never got used to.*

"Aunt Carol, they are six, seven, and nine. They know not to go outside when—"

She cut me off a third time. "You have twenty minutes to get in the house and see to my children. If the police end up at my doorstep, you'd better go with them, because if I get hold of you, I'll choke your ass out...I *mean* it!" she threatened before the line went dead.

I looked around at the few pairs of eyes watching me. They quickly looked away and went back to their own computers. Embarrassed, I immediately stood up, grabbed my schoolbag and got out of there as fast as I could.

Once upon a time, my aunt was nice. I have five aunts, and Aunt Carol was always my favorite. She was the most fun. She kept me laughing and would take me everywhere with her when my mother allowed me to go. Her three sons, Michael, James, and Jacob, were three mischievous little hoodlums, but you couldn't tell *her* that. They destroyed people's property, wet the bed, disrespected authority, and constantly started fights with the neighborhood kids. They were little liars and thieves, too. Their bedrooms were vile, filled with broken toys, dirty laundry thrown everywhere, and dirty dishes with old food crusting the bases. As soon as you walked into one of their rooms, you were overwhelmed by the reek of urine.

Actually, Aunt Carol's entire house was disgusting. Her furniture was badly stained and ripped on the seats. Her once beautiful plush white carpet was now a dingy gray color. The walls were full of graffiti from crayons and markers, and there were big holes caved into them from my cousins pretend wrestling matches.

Aunt Carol owned a dog and two cats, and it seemed as if the floor was their litter box. I'd lost count of how many times I'd stepped in cat poop in the living room. Some droppings had been there so long, they became a part of the rug.

Then, there was her big screen television that housed what seemed like a *million* roaches. Whenever we watched TV, they would crawl up the screen. There were bugs in every part of her house, and when the lights went out, they'd all come out to play. The moment the lights came on, hundreds of them scattered into cabinets, under the stove, into the walls, and underneath doors. The place looked like the inside of a dumpster.

Still, she would always exaggerate how extravagant her home was, and what angels her boys were. They could do no wrong. No fights, arguments, or properties destroyed were ever a result of them.

My mother couldn't stand Aunt Carol because she smoked cigarettes and cursed like a sailor, but she had the highest income out of her sisters at

$25,000 a year as a cook at the Marriott Hotel. She also had an associate's degree in business, which gave her the title of the most educated family member. My mom hated her for it, but not me. I loved my aunt more than anything...or at least I used to.

Aunt Carol was about 5'5" with short hair, mocha skin, and a size eight figure. She was married, at one point, to my Uncle Greg. Both of them were fun to be around, but they ended up separating. One night, they got into a heated argument, and he beat her so bad her face was barely recognizable. Greg added salt to the wound by throwing Aunt Carol down the living room steps. I was only about eight years old when this happened. I remember being at home with my mom when one of my aunts called with the news. My mother left me in the house, alone, to meet up with her sisters and about fifteen of my male cousins. They found my uncle and beat him up, almost to the point of death, as I later heard.

I was relieved when my mother signed over her parental rights. Aunt Carol took me in with open arms. There was no doubt in my mind that living with her would be so much fun since we had such good times when I was growing up. Once I moved in, however, all those good times soon became a blur as each memory faded away and was replaced with the *real* Aunt Carol. She and my mother were a lot alike. Aunt Carol was as mean as a junkyard dog. She treated me as if I were a live-in babysitter. Hell, I watched my cousins so much it was like they were my own kids. Aunt Carol constantly cursed me out and disrespected me. *Fat Ass* and *Pig* seemed to replace my real name.

Her newest boyfriend, Steven, also lived there. He was a major downgrade compared to Uncle Greg. Steve was even more of a jerk than Aunt Carol. I shared a room with his daughter, Chantal, who was a few years younger than me.

I'd been living with them for about 3 years, and I *hated* it. I would've rather gone into foster care than be there with them.

As the bus neared my stop, I dreaded having to get off. Reaching above my head, I pulled the string to alert the driver.

"Thanks," I said as I walked passed him and got off the bus. My cousins must have gone back into the house because there was no one on our street when I turned onto it.

I walked inside the house and there were my three cousins, running around. As soon as they heard the door open, they stopped and looked toward it. When they saw my face, their eyes widened, and their jaws dropped.

"OH, you're in *trouble*," Jacob teased.

"Steve is here waiting for you," Michael added. "You're going to *get it* now."

The moment he said that, James, the oldest one, went stampeding up the stairs.

"Steve!" he called out, "Mystery is *hooome.*"

Those little kids loved trouble and made sure to tell *every little thing*—except the things they did themselves.

"Mystery." The deep, baritone voice sent a flutter to my gut. "Get up here *now.*"

The boys watched and snickered as I put my bag down and walked up the steps to my aunt's room where Steve was.

"Yes," I said softly.

"Close the door." His stern, unforgiving voice brooded like a backdrop for a funeral.

I slowly closed the door and before I could even turn back around to face him, he forcefully pushed me across the room, sending me flying to the floor. My head slammed against the doorframe.

"I left work and missed out on my money, fucking around with your dumb ass," he hollered. "Where the hell were you?!"

Anger surged through my body like electricity, but I refused to answer him. I couldn't believe he'd pushed me like that.

"Hello?" he snapped.

The more my anger grew, the lower my eyebrows dipped, causing my forehead to crease. My lips curled, and my jaws clamped shut as I held the side of my head in pain while tears fell from my face. As soon as I used the back of my hand to wipe them away, a wooden hockey stick came swinging in my direction. Before I had the chance to react, it hit me. I hissed in pain, quickly grabbing my arm when it connected.

Steve struck me again, and again, and again... *and again*. He didn't care where he hit me—my leg, my back, my knee...he even hit me on the top of my shoulder blade, just missing my face. He hit me with the hockey stick, and periodically kicked me with his feet. My attempts to block his hits were useless, so I just slid to the floor and sheltered my head with my arms. The hits were too quick and too painful for me to do anything.

"Bitch, *answer* me when I'm talking to you," he fussed, continuing to swing my cousin's hockey stick.

"The next time you pull a stunt like this, I'll kill you. You don't pay bills here—*we do*." His words penetrated with each hit. "If you're gonna live here, then you're gonna follow *our* rules, or get the fuck out. You hear me?"

"Yes!" I screamed. "Just stop hitting me."

I thought I was gonna die. Steve was well over three hundred pounds and had the strength of two linebackers. He swung the hockey stick like he was trying to score the winning goal during a hockey match, and I was the opposing goalie who stood in his way. My entire body was on fire, and I was worried he had broken some of my bones—it certainly felt like he had.

"Stop. Stop!" I screamed. My pleas did nothing.

"I'll stop when I *feel* like stopping, just like you couldn't come home in time to get the boys because you didn't *feel* like it, right?" he taunted.

I didn't know how long the beating went on for, but I felt a softer kick from his size thirteen boot and heard the sound of the hockey stick hitting the floor, signaling it was over.

Steve took a deep breath and used his other foot to kick me one last time. "Now get the hell out of my face."

I stood up as fast as my aching body would allow me to and snatched the door open. I felt like a slave breaking free as I crossed the threshold of the doorway, but after taking three steps into the hallway, my body gave out. I fell to my knees in agony, sobbing on the way to the floor. It hurt too much to move, but I was on a mission to get the hell away from my aunt's door before her boyfriend came back out and decided to hit me again.

My room was only a few feet away. I looked up at my door and began crawling toward my bedroom. When I made it through the door, I closed it and curled into a fetal position on the floor. My body tightened up, and I felt light-headed. I lay on the floor a few more minutes before attempting to get in my bed. Using the wall as leverage, I pulled myself up from the hardwood floor. Instantly, the room started to spin, and everything went black as I fainted.

Chapter 3

A cold splash of water jolted me out of a very turbulent unconscious, feeling like I'd been smashed in the chest. That second you remember where you are and why, is the hardest. Aunt Carol stood over me with a plastic cup in one hand and the other planted on her hip. The look of concern and fear was evident in her eyes. I think she thought I was dead at first until I came to; after that her expression changed right back into the villainous monster she was.

"You woke?" her cold, pitiless tone enquired.

"I'm woke," I muttered.

"Get up and get downstairs. Dinner is ready."

I felt her eyes staring at me as I struggled to get up, a throbbing surge of torment lit my body up like a Christmas tree. Using the ladder from the bunk bed in my room, I stood up. Aunt Carol stood there and watched as I limped past her to walk toward the steps.

"How was counseling?" she asked.

Steve came out of the bedroom and looked over the banister.

"Great," I muttered without looking back. *I couldn't stand either of them.*

"See, she's good," I heard Steve whisper to my aunt. "She's a big girl. I didn't hurt her *that* bad."

"Big girl or not, you shouldn't have hit her with a *hockey stick*. You break a bone or leave a mark bad enough to send her to the hospital, then what?

You think she's gonna lie and say she fell? *No.* She's going to tell the truth, and then that's my ass in questioning," she scolded, irritated. "I get a check from the state for her, I don't need anything messing up my money."

"Well how about the next time the kids are left unattended, *you* leave work and miss out on your own money instead of asking me to do it," Steve fussed back. "Mystery's good. She can walk, she's breathing...but she deserved it. Her fat ass needs to learn some respect for authority."

"By all means, beat her, but not with a *hockey stick.* That's all I'm saying." Both of them walked down the steps behind me, talking about me like I couldn't hear them.

Walking into the kitchen, I sat down in front of my food. I didn't want to eat. I wanted to take some medicine and go to sleep. I could barely sit down at the dinner table without wincing, and my upper arm pulsated each time I lifted my spoon. My cousins kept glancing over at me. They didn't even try to hide their snickers.

*****

The next morning, I made an attempt to stretch my aching arms as I walked toward my closet door and peered inside to search for something cute to wear to school. I had absolutely no fashion sense. Growing up, my mother never taught me about style. I didn't know how to do my hair, how to shop for myself, or how to coordinate an outfit. She always did my hair the way she insisted and dressed me the way she wanted me to look. Now that I was on my own, I just wore what was comfortable. I owned five pairs of baggy men's jeans, five t-shirts, and a pair of timberland boots. I wanted to make a good impression as an 11th grader, but this wardrobe certainly wouldn't get the job done. I backed away from my closet door and went into the bathroom to fix my hair. My usual ponytail took no time at all. After grabbing the hair gel from the mirrored cabinet above the sink, I closed it and took a look at myself. A few seconds later, I looked away in shame. At fifteen, I was well over the average weight for my age. I hated the heavyset, dark-skinned reflection that stared back at me. Being big-boned had always been an issue for me, and my mother hated it.

"You *are* a pig," I could hear her voice echoing in my thoughts. "You are a fat, black, pig. Nobody wants you and nobody will ever love you until you lose some weight." She never missed an opportunity to wound and criticize me. *And wound they did.* I was fifteen years old and hated the way I looked. Growing up, my mother would try to control my weight by punishing me with starvation. She fed me ramen noodles and cream of wheat in small portions a few times per day. I always woke up hungry and went to bed starving. At one point, my eight-year-old mind conjured up the idea of committing a crime bad enough to be sent to prison. At least there, the prisoners were fed three meals a day. After moving in with Aunt Carol, I was free to eat what I wanted, whenever I wanted to, *and so it began.* Every chance I got, I binged on ridiculous amounts of food in large portions, subconsciously hoarding food just in case I ever ran into someone who would deny me my freedom to eat. Within two years, I gained so much weight, I looked like the goodyear blimp.

After fixing my hair and brushing my teeth, I went back into my room to get dressed. I looked ridiculous. Nothing about me said pretty, especially compared to my favorite cousin, Autumn. We went to the same school. She was my Aunt Ethel's daughter, and out of all of my cousins, we were the closest. Even though she was a year older than me, we were in the same grade because she'd been held back a year. Years ago, my mother would take me to Autumn's house before she went to work in the mornings. Autumn and I would play Barbie dolls and dress-up until it was time for me to go home.

Autumn was beautiful—slim, with a gorgeous earth-toned complexion that reflected her name. With her petite size zero figure, she always made a statement with her endless wardrobe.

Autumn always had something creative going on with her hair. At sixteen, she was one of the most beautiful eleventh graders in the neighborhood. I wanted to be just like her. I never had an identity of my own other than the one my mother had given me, and now that she was out of the picture I had no clue who I was. I dreamed of being like every thin, light skinned pretty girl with a mother who loved them. Growing up, I always lived in my imagination for comfort. I called myself Jessica and was happiest living vicariously aboard a beautiful motherless cruise ship with a nanny who loved me, and a dog named pepper. I pretended that I was Michelle from full house, and Olivia from the Cosby's. I saw myself living with the Fresh prince in Belaire, safe and warm, tucked away with people who loved me. I mothered my dolls the way I longed to be nurtured. I carried them around, showering them with love and attention, making sure they were safe. I remember mothering myself, imagining that I'd been switched at birth and given to the wrong mother. I told myself that my real mom would come and find me someday. I knew all along that the mother I had was the one I had been born to, but it felt safe to pretend like the journey of torture would end at some point.

After grabbing my backpack, I limped downstairs and out of the front door to meet Autumn. As soon as I reached the end of the block, I could see her bouncy weave and pink pencil skirt walking in my direction.

"Missy!" she yelled.

She scurried the rest of the way to meet me. As soon as she got close enough, she gave me a big hug. Even her frail arms hugging me sent painful shocks through my arms and down my chest from the beating I'd taken from Steve. Instantly, I jerked away from the pain. My reaction must have startled her. Autumn pulled back and looked at me, her eyebrows furrowing.

"What's the matter with you?" She laughed. "I showered this morning, so I know I don't stink."

"Hey." I offered a slight smile and we started our walk to school. "It's not you. My body hurts. How are you? What did you do last night?"

"Nothing much," she shrugged. "Cooked dinner and talked on the phone with Kevin." She blushed as she reached for her cellphone to check her text messages.

"Autumn, its seven thirty in the morning—Kevin is not texting you this early."

"You don't know that," she chuckled. "I texted him good morning when I woke up, and I'm waiting for him to respond."

"Oh my God," I laughed. "We all go to the same school, and we're in the *same* class. Why can't you just wait until you see each other?"

"You're too young to understand grown folks' business," she responded playfully. "Today, Kevin and the rest of the football team are opening up the pep rally in the school yard, so we can't miss them. I can't *wait* to see my baby."

"The baby you talked to until six this morning and then texted at six fifteen...and are now rushing to get to at seven thirty?" We both laughed.

As we continued to walk to school, my legs began to hurt. Slowing my pace, I started trailing behind.

"You're walking so slow. Come on, we need to get to the school yard."

"Hang on, my legs are really sore." I stopped walking and winced in pain. My muscles had tightened up.

"What in the *world* is wrong with you? Why are you in so much pain?"

"If I tell you something, you have to promise not to say anything to anyone."

Her eyes lit up. "You lost your virginity?" Her mouth formed into a wide grin as she squealed in excitement.

"What? No." I sucked my teeth. "And I hope losing my virginity doesn't involve being bruised up like I am. If so, I'm keeping it forever."

"Bruised up?" Her eyebrow raised.

"Mr. Steve and Aunt Carol got upset because I went to the library after counseling yesterday and I forgot to call them. I didn't think it was a big deal. She got pissed because the boys were home alone, and Steve had to leave work early. When I got there, he cursed me out and beat me up with Jacob's hockey stick."

The look of shock registered on Autumn's face before she could respond. "Are you serious? That's *awful*! I'm telling my mom."

"No," I said quickly. "Don't say anything. Aunt Carol will get angry and make me leave. I don't have any place else to go."

"That's crazy, Mystery. A *hockey stick*? Are you hurt bad?"

"My body is *killing* me. He hit me everywhere, as hard as he could. I have welts and bruises all over," I shook my head.as we began to walk again. "I wish I could go live with my dad."

"Is he still in jail for child support?" Autumn asked.

"No, he got out a few months ago, but the judge ordered him to a halfway house until he gets on his feet because he was on drugs when they locked him up. If he can stay clean, they'll allow him his parental rights back. Who knows if that'll ever happen."

Autumn shook her head. "I'd have chosen to go into foster care rather than deal with Aunt Carol and her devil of a boyfriend."

"The judge *wanted* to put me in foster care, but Aunt Carol stood up for me and told the judge she didn't want me to get lost in the system. She told them she loved me and wanted me to have a fair chance."

"Well this certainly isn't a fair chance." Autumn shook her head. "She just wanted a check."

"Maybe I could stay with you," I suggested hopefully. "If your mom will let me."

"Yeah right, I wish. There are ten of us in a three-bedroom house. After she took in Aunt Gwen's kids, my mom can't afford another mouth to feed," Autumn said.

"I understand," I replied with my head hung low. "I'm just going to ride it out. Hopefully things will get better."

As we approached our high school, all the football players were going into the yard for the pep rally.

"You can go ahead," I said to Autumn, "I'm going to homeroom. I don't feel like standing."

"Okay," she said in a low voice. "I'll see you at lunch. Hope you feel better. Go to the nurse and ask for Motrin if you're still hurting like that."

"I will," I responded.

Chapter 4

I sat in the back of my math class doodling in my journal, periodically glancing at the clock above the chalkboard.

"Guys, it's almost time to go. Pass up your homework assignments and copy tonight's homework from the board, please," Ms. Stokes said.

Everyone passed up an assignment but me. I never did homework. I barely did *any* assigned work.

"Missy, where's your homework?" Ms. Stokes walked toward me with her arms folded.

"If I didn't pass it up, I must not have done it."

The *nerve* of her putting me on blast in front of the class. Offended, I stared her down with cold eyes.

"This is the fourth time this week you've failed to do homework." She entered my personal space, hovering above me.

"Okay...and tomorrow will be the fifth. What's your point?"

"I want to talk to you after school" she replied, locking her eyes on me with a look of disappointment.

"No thank you. I have places to go."

I packed my schoolbag just as the bell rang for dismissal. Ms. Stokes turned around to the rest of the class.

"Don't forget to read chapter six tonight. Everyone have a good evening. You're dismissed."

She turned back around to face me. "Not you," she said firmly as I got up from my seat to leave.

"Oh my God, *come on.*" Rolling my eyes, I huffed, "I have to go."

"Is everything all right at home?" she asked with a look of concern.

"Is everything all right at *your* home?" I shot back quickly.

"I'm serious. You seem like such a bright girl, yet you only do enough work to pass. You always sit toward the back, and you always have a nasty attitude, like you're pissed to be alive. What is the problem?"

"The problem is...you're in my face, you're in my business, and now you're wasting my time." I swung my backpack over my shoulder and brushed past her to get to the door.

"Okay, you know what? If you don't turn in your homework or any assignments tomorrow, I'm sending you to in-school suspension for all of next week," she fussed.

"Who cares?" I mumbled, storming out of the classroom.

"*And* I'm calling a parent-teacher conference," she hollered out the door.

"Good luck with that," I hollered back, laughing sarcastically.

I hated teachers. If it weren't for Autumn and being able to get away from home, I'd never come to school. School work was always the last thing on my mind. I had other important things to think about at fifteen years old; *how many times will Aunt Carol call me names today? Will her boyfriend knock me upside my head tonight? Will I be able to sit with myself for a moment of solace, or will I be stuck babysitting? Will I ever see my dad again? Will I ever lose weight? How much longer do I have to live in this cruel world? When will it be my time to die so I can finally rest in peace?"* As I walked out of the building toward the bus stop, I pulled out my phone to text my aunt to let her know I was on my way to counseling. I hated that I had to check in with her; it wasn't like she cared anyway.

The bus pulled up just as I reached the stop. The driver opened the door and I stepped inside. I put my school token in and made my way to the back to sit down. On the way to my seat, I walked past a little girl who looked to be about nine or ten years old, sitting next to her mother. The woman had her arms wrapped around her daughter as they laughed and talked. I found a window seat a few rows behind them and sat down. I watched as the little girl told her mother a story. Her face was flushed as she giggled, reminiscing about a boy she liked. Her mother looked on in amusement, tilting her head back in laughter. That made me smile. I had an obsession with seeing mothers and daughters together. I watched them in the supermarket aisles or riding bikes in the park. I studied them in the Laundromat, and during parent teacher report card conferences- and was all the more bewildered. Why were my mother and I so different? I felt so alone. I thought I was the only girl in the world born to a mother who didn't love her. The mothers I read about in books and saw on television were nothing like mine. I envied my cousins for the mothers they had. I wanted to be like Autumn, whose mother was thoughtful and attentive, or my other cousin Victoria, whose mother told her funny stories and allowed us to make a mess in her kitchen when we baked a cake from scratch. Why didn't my mother love me the way she was supposed to? Whose fault was it? Mine or hers?

I remembered hearing stories from various family members that my mother began abusing me when I was just two weeks old. My cries for attention, food and to be held irritated her so much that instead of picking me up, she would pinch me in an attempt to shut me up.

As I listened to the little girl in front of me continue on about her crush, happy and carefree, my mind began to drift back to when I was her age. That season of my life was anything but happy and carefree. We lived with my grandmother Elaine, and my Aunt Gwen at the time. I recalled a time when my mother walked into the house from work as I sat on the floor watching TV while my aunt sat on the couch reading a magazine.

"Mommy," I hollered in excitement and jumped up to greet her. Stretching out my arms, I raced over and tried to hug her, but before I could get to her, she extended her arm and pushed me back, sending me flying into the wall.

"Get away from me," she scolded. "It's ninety-five degrees outside and I'm sweating. It's too hot to be touched."

The back of my head hit the banister. I grabbed it, sliding to the floor in pain.

"Did you seriously just push her like that?" Aunt Gwen dropped her magazine and rushed to see about me. She kneeled to the floor to touch my head. I screamed.

"She's being dramatic, and you're egging her on," My mom shook her head and walked into the living room. "She's fine."

"No. She has a knot on the back of her head now," Aunt Gwen explained as she helped me up. "Come on Missy, let's go get you some ice."

"Leave her alone," my mom shouted back as she turned around, approaching the hallway where we were. "I *said* she was fine."

"I don't care *what* you said," Aunt Gwen hissed.

"This is my child." My mom pointed at me.

"There's plenty of children in the world with mothers that don't deserve them. Your psychotic ass is one of them!" she hollered.

"Mystery, let's go. We're leaving." My mom yanked me away from Aunt Gwen's grasp.

"At least take some ice for her head," Aunt Gwen looked concerned.

"I'm so sick of you and everyone else telling me how to raise my child. If you want kids so bad, stop aborting them," my mother fired back. "You're the reason why I'm moving out now. I'm in the process of getting my own place so I can raise my daughter in peace."

"Oh, she's your *daughter* now? Yesterday you told her she was the worst mistake of your life, and the day before that she was your worst nightmare and you wished her dead. Now all of a sudden she's your daughter and the rest of us are the bad guys?" Aunt Gwen shook her head. "You need help."

"It's people like you who pay so much attention to everybody else's situation but can never turn a mirror on themselves," my mom told her.

"Oh, go to hell," Aunt Gwen hissed.

"*It's my second home,*" my mom responded coldly. She rolled her eyes, grabbed me by the arm, and walked out the door.

"You're a disgrace to society," Aunt Gwen said just before slamming the door behind us.

"Get in the car, *now.*" My mom unlocked the door and got in on the driver's side. I got in the front seat and closed the door. I turned to the right to get my seatbelt, but when I turned to the left to fasten it, my mom's powerful fist met me instead.

"You see all the trouble you cause?" she scolded, punching me a second time. "I wish you'd just *die.*"

Her clenched teeth reminded me of an angry tiger we'd seen at the zoo. She continuously punched me in my chest and slapped me in the face. I tried shielding myself with my forearms, but she was too fast.

"There's nothing wrong with your head, but I'll make something wrong with it now."

She gripped the back of my neck with her right hand and slammed my forehead into the dashboard of the car. I hollered in agony as I felt the bridge of my nose snap. Instantly, I grabbed it. Blood began to leak out from my nose and run down my hands. Effortlessly and heartlessly, she'd broken my nose. *Just like that.*

Throughout the years, she planted seeds of disappointment and rage that blossomed at any given moment.

*****

My cellphone vibrating in my pocket interrupted my thoughts. Reaching for it, I saw that it was my grandmother calling.

"Hello?" I answered.

"Hey. How are you?" she said.

"I'm great, just out doing some stuff. What's up?"

"Nothing much. I have a surprise for you," she sounded excited.

"What is it?" I asked excitedly.

"Your mother is in town."

Chapter 5

"She's here until tomorrow night," my grand-mother continued as I walked toward my counselor's office. "She said she'd stop by Carol's to see you."

"I...I have school," I stuttered.

"Well you can miss *one* day. You haven't seen your mother in three years."

I held my phone to my ear and looked at the ground. I didn't have a rebuttal

"Great." My grandmother accepted my silence as a green light. "She'll be there between seven-thirty and eight in the morning."

"...All right," I responded hesitantly.

I said goodbye and ended the call just before walking into the big building at the end of the block. Getting on the elevator, I made my way to the 5th floor to see Dr. Robinson.

My heart beat so fast, I thought it would give away at any moment. *Why is my mom here, and what does she want from me?* Three years ago, I sat in my bedroom listening to her rant and rave about sleeping with a married deacon from our church. One Sunday morning, I walked into the church with my grandmother and my mother, eager to see who this mystery man was. As all of the deacons trolled the aisles passing the offering plate, I whispered to my grandmother, "where's Deacon Baxter?" I was horrified when she pointed out a man that looked to be in his mid to late sixties. I watched his wife walk over to my mother with the biggest smile on her face, excited to see her. I watched my mother's face light up like a kid on Christmas as she leaped up to hug her.

"Look at them," my grandmother smiled, "two peas in a pod."

"Do they know each other?" I asked.

"Do they? That's Deacon Baxter's wife. She's been like a second mother to your mother since she was born. She practically raised her while I worked nights and weekends at the hospital, and Deacon Baxter has always been so kind about it. Took her in like his own daughter."

I wasn't sure if that was the reason my mother referred to him as "daddy" over the phone, but I chose to sit back in my seat and mind my business for the remainder of the service. During the drive home, my mother threatened to whoop me after she saw me talking during service. She warned me about talking during church.

"Beat her for what?" My grandmother hissed, "She opened her mouth for two seconds to ask me who Deacon Baxter was." My mother slammed on the brakes so hard I nearly choked on my seatbelt. Thanks a lot grandma. My mother looked at me from her rearview mirror with eyes that resembled saucers. She knew in that moment that I'd been listening to her phone conversations. Stepping on the gas, she hightailed it to my grandmother's apartment building. When we got there, she practically threw her out of the car and waved goodbye. If I had known better I would've waved goodbye as well, because life as I knew it was getting ready to change. When we got home, she dragged me out of the car like a rag doll, accusing me of telling my grandmother and the whole church what she'd been doing. She tossed me into the house, pushed me into the carpet, and caved her foot into my chest. Picking me up, she threw me into the door and slapped me into the floor once more. She hit me so many times, I think I lost consciousness. I remember regaining it long enough to see her reach for her metal bat sitting by the wall. I saw her lift it, and then everything else went black. I woke up in the hospital fighting for my life, surrounded by police officers, and the department of child services. She moved to Arizona a few months after, leading me to believe that her reign of terror and emotional deprivation was over. *Why was she back?*

Stepping off the elevator, I slowly headed to the receptionist's desk, but before I could sign in, Dr. Robinson came out of her office.

"Hi there," her welcoming smile greeted me. "I just saw you on the camera getting off the elevator. Come on in." She motioned for me to follow her into her office. Once I walked in, she closed the door behind us.

"So how's it go—"

Before she could finish her sentence, I burst into tears.

"What's wrong?" She furrowed, "it down and talk to me."

I wanted to tell her about Steve, but he was the least of my worries right then. The devil was in town, headed for *my* house.

"My mother is coming." I sat down, wiping my falling tears.

"Coming here?" Her brow raised.

"No, to my aunt's house to see me in the morning.

"You look horrified." Dr. Robinson handed me some tissues from her desk.

"I don't want to see her," I lowered my head.

"Well, why subject yourself to something you don't want to do?"

"My grandmom asked me too."

"Does she know and understand the depth of the relationship between you two?" Dr. Robinson asked.

"Of course, she does," I gestured with my hands, "she doesn't care what kind of person her daughter amounted to. No matter what's happened, she always says *that's still your mother*, like I owe her something for giving me life."

"That's understandable."

"Well I'm glad you understand," I said, "because I don't get it at all."

"Cultural norms- backed by the Christian tradition requires us to honor our parents and to speak no ill of them," Dr. Robinson stated matter-of-factly. "In the court of the mother-daughter conflict, its usually the daughter who's on trial."

"Everyone that knows about my relationship with my mother seems to blame *me* and excuse *her*. That's not fair," my tear strained eyes looked up.

"It's not fair at all," Dr. Robinson agreed. "There was no one in your life to advocate for you? What about school officials? Parents of your friends? Did you ever reach out for help?"

"No," I replied somberly. "My mom was a charming and beautiful woman who stepped into the world with the highest of heels, and bright, shiny jewelry on her hands and neck. There wasn't so much as a strand of hair out of place. She flirted with everyone, and everyone found her to be delightful. Who would've believed me?" Dr. Robinson takes notes as I talk.

"You mentioned she resented you for your dark features. How did she treat you in public?"

"I grew into my looks, and eventually it worked in her favor," I responded. "I had a head full of curly hair and dark skin that was so radiant, I remember people stopping to stare on the street as they walked by. My mom accented my looks with beautiful clothes and hair accessories. *I looked like a doll baby.* I received a lot of attention and praise from outsiders. I was a project to her. I earned her accolades, praise, and a lot of attention from everyone around us. People were dying to know her secret for such good parenting. In the public's eye, she was a living Mary Poppins. Behind closed doors, she was something out of a horror film."

"How did you feel as all of this took place? Were you afraid?"

"I was very afraid," I nodded, "but I thought fear was normal. I assumed everyone was afraid of their mother. I didn't have any siblings to talk to, or close friends to compare childhoods with. When I was about nine years old, we moved out of my grandmother's house and into a two-bedroom apartment. *And her reign of terror began.* She kept me confined to my bedroom, forced to sit on the edge of the bed and stare at the walls. I had toys I was never allowed to touch- they were only for show- to be seen and admired by guests who came over once in a while, to convince them she was a good mother. I wasn't allowed to watch TV, or roam around our apartment freely. I needed her permission to go to the bathroom, or to get water from the kitchen. I was only allowed to eat when she fed me, which was twice a day. She gave me cream of wheat for breakfast, and ramen noodles for dinner. I hated cream of wheat, but I didn't have choices, so I learned to like it."

Dr. Robinson stared at me. I think she wanted to say something, or jot my confession down in her notes, but she was at a loss for words. All she could do was allow me the floor, so I could continue.

"During the summer time when there was no school and I couldn't go to Autumn's house, my mother would lock me in my bedroom for the day," my voice shook, recalling the horrible memories that still terrified me at times. "She would leave a bucket in my bedroom filled with bleach and water for me to use the bathroom, and then she'd walk out and padlock the door from the outside, so I couldn't get out. Sometimes, she didn't lock it," I recalled. "Sometimes she left my door open and dared me to walk out of it. She told me if I stepped foot into the hallway she'd know, and she'd beat me when she got home. I remember days where I'd sit on my bed starving, staring out into the hallway. All I had to do was walk out and go downstairs for a slice of bread, but I was so terrified that she would find out, I'd just sit on my bed and stare at the stairwell, too scared to walk out.

"Did your mother hit you often?"

"She hit me until I bled. Until lumps formed, and my skin turned blue and purple. She hit me with belts, extension cords, brushes, cable cords, and her pocketbook straps. She beat me across my back, my legs, my arms- anywhere she could. She threw me down stairs, blackened my eyes, cut me with knives, stuck me in ovens, and burned my hands on the stove. She was the bullet I couldn't dodge, and gunfire would come from anywhere. She never hugged or kissed me. I can remember countless times when I told her I loved her, and she ignored me. I was never allowed to touch her- she didn't like to be touched. She never looked directly at me unless she was beating me up. Still, I wanted to be around her. Her power was so enormous. She was the sun, and I needed her light more than anything in the world, but she kept me in the dark. I was forced to live in her shadows. She scarred my body, and scarred my heart, but I loved my mother just as much as I feared her. I wanted her affection and attention just as much as I wanted to be able to answer the question I couldn't answer as a child and now a teenager: Why doesn't she love me?"

Chapter 6

Later that night

"Are you okay?" Autumn asked me through the phone. I lay in my bed on my stomach, staring at the floor.

"Yeah," I replied, "just ready to get tomorrow over with." There was a brief silence on the other end of the phone before Autumn replied with,

"I'm so sorry you have to go through so much." She wanted so badly to help, but there was nothing she could do. "Listen, I have to go, it's almost midnight. Please call me as soon as you get away from her, so I know you're still *alive* at least."

"I will. Good night."

I hung up the phone and put it on the pillow beside me. I was so tired, but my thoughts refused to let my mind calm down enough for me to sleep. Steve's daughter was on the top bunk snoring, so that didn't help either. I went to reach for my phone again, but before I could get it, a large figure crept into my room and crawled into my bed, slithering its way to my face. It was Steve. Gasping loudly, I tried to scream, but he quickly put his hand over my mouth.

"Calm down," he gritted. "You're gonna wake up the whole house."

The scent of beer invaded my nostrils from his hand. He was drunk...*again*. The light from my cellphone cast a dim blue light over his face, and the twisted spark in his eye told me something bad was going to happen. Steve hovered closely over me, gazing into my eyes as if it were normal.

"What do you want?" I mumbled under his hand.

"I was walking past and heard you in here talking." He slowly moved his hand. "Who were you talking to?"

"*What do you want?*" I ignored his question.

His eyes rolled down to my breasts as if he could see through the t-shirt I was wearing, and then he looked back up at me.

"Let me ask you something, Missy," he slurred, "are you still a virgin?"

"*What?*"

Steve put his hands under the covers and started to feel his way up my leg. My eyes grew big, and I tried to push him away.

"Don't act like you don't want it." He knocked my arm out of the way. Using his free hand, he gripped me by the neck.

"Get *off* of me," I fussed loudly, not caring about any of his threats.

He quickly moved his hand and put it back over my mouth. "Didn't I tell you to shut the *fuck* up?"

His voice was low and raspy, but loud enough for me to hear him.

The bed above us squeaked from his daughter moving.

"Missy?" Chantal called from the top bunk

Steve quickly got up, stumbling as fast as he could out of the room.

"Yes?" I answered, trying to sound as normal as possible.

"What was that?" She peeked her head down to see me. "Were you talking to someone, or were you dreaming?"

"It was just a bad dream," I swallowed, terrified.

"You okay?"

"I'm fine," I told her. "Go back to bed."

When her head disappeared back into her bed, I let the tears building up in my eyes fall down the sides of my face.

What the heck just happened? At that point, I wished I *had* been dreaming. My heart was doing backflips in my chest. Quickly, I got up from the bed and locked the bedroom door, so he couldn't come back to finish what he started. I climbed back into my bed, pulled the cover all the way up to my chin, and kept my eyes on the door until they could no longer stay open.

Chapter 7

My alarm clock went off shortly after six the next morning. As soon as I managed to open my eyes, I felt a headache surge to the forefront of my head. I got up, walked over to my alarm, and cut it off. I hadn't slept much during the night, too afraid of Steve coming back into my room. I walked back over to the bed and sat down. Taking a few moments to get myself together, I looked around. I was mentally exhausted.

My mother stole my childhood, her sister was stealing my teenage years, and now her boyfriend was trying to steal my virginity.

I got up, took off my pajamas, wrapped my pink towel around my body, and walked into the bathroom to get into the shower. Before I could even turn on the faucet, someone began to bang on the door.

"Missy!" Steve hollered. "Get out of the bathroom, I've got to get in there. I'm running late."

The moment I heard his voice, I was instantly annoyed. I didn't bother to answer him.

"Little girl, I know you're in there," he yelled. "Get out the damn—"

Rolling my eyes, I secured my towel and opened the bathroom door. As soon as I stepped out, Steve yanked my arm, pulling me the rest of the way into the hallway. The force from his football player arms sent my head soaring into the wall. I could've blocked the impact with my arms but holding on to my towel was more important. My face hit the wall. I turned around to face him. If looks could kill, he would've dropped dead.

"Stop putting your hands on me," I hissed. "Stop touching me, stop hitting me, and stop looking at me you fucking pedophile!"

The words flew from my mouth before I could think about what I was saying.

Steve glared at me in complete and utter disbelief at my big mouth.

"Are you crazy?" he threatened.

"I'm not crazy, but you're a child abuser and a child molest-" a punch in the stomach stopped me in mid-sentence. I fell to the ground, gripping my body as Steve began to kick me like a soccer ball.

"Stop hitting me!" I screamed. "Get *off* me."

Aunt Carol came running out of the bedroom to stop him.

"Steve, what are you doing?" She grabbed him. "You're going to kill her."

He stopped his attack and looked down at me, taking in deep, heavy breaths.

"He came into my room last night drunk and tried to rape me" I cried out in defense.

My cousins opened their doors to see what the problem was.

"Whatever, she's a liar. Her fat ass walked in on me while I was in the bathroom. She took her towel off and pranced around in here asking me to sleep with her, "he spat. "She did the same thing last night, before you got home." Aunt Carol snapped her head in my direction. "I will beat her to *death* if she disrespects my house and our relationship like this again. She has to go, Carol. I won't stand for this!"

Did he really just lie like that? I was fuming as I gathered my towel and tried to stand up, but my Aunt Carol kicked me back down.

"You...did *what?*" She glared me, looking like the epitome of everything that was evil.

"He's lying," I shouted. "I was getting ready to take my—"

Before I could finish my sentence, my aunt began wailing on me. I tried to shield my face and crawl away, but I was unsuccessful. Her kicks were too fast, her punches too hard.

"This is the thanks I get after I let you come stay in my house? Really? *Really!*"

"I didn't do anything, Aunt Carol. He's lying."

My cousins all ran over to try to pull my aunt off of me, but nobody could stop her. Steve stood back and watched with a smirk on his face.

"You ain't shit, and you'll never be nothing but a bitch like your mother. I could've just left your ass to the state. How *dare* you? In *my* house?" She continued to swing on me. "You fat, nasty slob. My man doesn't want you. *No man does.* Get your shit and get out."

My cousins were finally able to pull her off of me...and thank God, too, because if she kept hitting me, I was certain she would've killed me.

"Matter of fact, forget your belongings. Just get out, and don't come back! Kill yourself for all I care." She pointed at the stairs.

Her eyes were bloodshot red, and her hair was all over her head. She looked like something out of The Exorcist.

I sat up on the floor, humiliated and hurt. Steve grabbed me by the arms and dragged me down the steps.

"Get her out of here," my aunt shouted.

"I need to get my clothes," I cried.

"You're not getting shit," he teased. "Your big mouth is going to get you killed one day."

Steve continued to push and pull me to the front door. "But for now, it just got you kicked out. You're going to regret the day you ain't give me no ass," he mumbled.

Steve opened up the front door and pushed me out. With my hands clenched to my side, I held my towel around my beaten body. There were no shoes on my feet, nor any clothes to put on my back. It was almost seven AM, and I stood outside of my aunt's house practically nude. I had no phone, and nowhere to go. I walked into a nearby alleyway and stepped in the dirty sewer water. Pressing up against the wall, I buried my face in my hands, melted down onto the dirty ground, and began to cry.

"Mystery," a stern, cold voice called from a few feet away.

I turned toward it, instantly freezing when I saw my mother standing there with her arms folded across her chest.

Chapter 8

Gathering my towel, I stared at the ground, embarrassed. This was not how I expected to see my mother after three years.

"Hello," I said.

"Hello to you," She replied. "You're still the same ol' Mystery—always in the midst of something messy. What happened *this* time?" she asked.

"It wasn't me, and I—"

"Blah blah, same old sad song. It's never you, always somebody else, right?" she teased.

"Do you mind taking me to Grandma's house? Aunt Carol just threw me out, and I'm here in a towel." Standing up, I rewrapped my towel.

"Absolutely not," She sneered. "My mother doesn't want you. She's getting too old to be dealing with such a problem child. I can't think of anyone else in this family that can stomach you, either-except your lowlife father. How about I drop you off there? Do you even know where he lives?" She laughed coldly.

"He lives in uptown with his girlfriend, but I haven't spoken to him in a long time," I said.

"Of course not. The courts informed him that you were living with your aunt and that he could take you back when he wanted to, he just didn't want you. Nobody does," she sneered. Seeing me in such a fragile state seemed to give her joy. She never missed an opportunity to wound or criticize me. She loved to kick me while I was down and tell me how useless I was to this world.

"What's your point? What do you want? Why are you here?" I snapped my head up at her.

"I came to see your grandmother, actually, and she begged me to come see you...so I'm here. Get in the car, since you don't have your father's address I'll take you to a shelter." She turned to walk to her car.

I didn't want to go with her, as much as I did want to go with her. I was so afraid of her, yet, I loved her so much. My life had just taken a turn for the worst, and she'd been right there to see it. Deep down, I hoped she'd take me into her arms and drive me to safety instead of a shelter. Maybe she would agree to get herself together and learn to mother me and love me. I would've been patient with her, but that wasn't going to happen.

I quickly followed her to her car and got in on the passenger side. She started the engine and pulled out of the parking space.

"I would offer you some breakfast, but you look like you've been eating too much breakfast already." She reared her head back and laughed at her insult. "You've gotten so fat, *wow*—you look like a Christmas turkey."

"Why do you hate me so much?" I turned to her. "What did I do to you?"

"Mystery, I don't hate you," she explained. "Your father was supposed to be around to help take care of you, but he didn't want anything to do with me, and I didn't have the money to get rid of you, so... here you are." She shrugged. "I tried to be the best mother I could be, but you refused to take heed. You went to your school nurse and told her you were afraid to come back home. Congrats—you wanted out, they took you out, and now you will forever pay the price for it. Nobody wants someone else's *burden*, and that's what you are. Nobody will ever love and care for you like your mother."

"Love and care?" I repeated the foreign words. "When you left, you didn't speak to me at all. You told me you weren't my mother anymore so there was no reason to call you mom. You'd call Aunt Carol for the holidays, excited to talk to the boys, but when she gave me the phone, you'd hang up on me. You've never called to wish me happy birthday, happy New Year, Merry Christmas, nothing. That's not love and care."

"That's your fault. *You* picked your poison. I didn't tell you to leave, *you left*. So what if I didn't want you? I took care of you. You made the mistake of leaving *me*, thinking the grass was greener on the other side. Newsflash, it isn't."

My eyes filled with tears and my heart filled with anger. She was right.

"I'm doing great in Arizona," she continued. "I have a good job, a white boyfriend, a new car, and no kids."

"All right," I snapped. "Just let me out at this light," I ordered. "I've heard enough."

"No. You asked me a question, and I'll let you out when I'm finished answering it," she said sternly. "You chose this life, not—"

Before she could finish her sentence, I punched her in the side of her temple as hard as I could. I couldn't take her honesty anymore. I had been through enough the previous night and that

47

morning. The punch seemed to hurt my hand more than my mother because she didn't even flinch. She slammed on the brakes in the middle of the intersection and put the car in park. She turned to me with a grimacing stare, grabbing my neck with one hand and my hair by the other.

"Have you lost your *mind?* I'm still your mother, and you *will* respect me as such."

The grip she had on my neck tightened. I wanted to fight back, but I couldn't. As she stared at me, choking the life out of me, I felt helpless. She was right: she *was* my mother, and I loved her. I wanted a relationship with her, but I knew it would never happen. This was the only part of her I would ever see. She let go of my neck and my hair. I grabbed at my throat, gasping for air.

"Get out of my car!" she screamed. "Get out of my life."

Before I turned to get out, she spit in my face. I quickly jerked back in disgust.

"You're garbage. Get *out.*"

Still gripping my towel, I quickly opened up the car door. I got out and slammed it shut just as her tires screeched and she pulled off. Where was I going to go? There was no one for me to call and she had driven too far for me to know where I was. I walked across the street into a nearby alleyway, wiping the spit from my face. The dirty water from the ground splashed all over my legs and my feet as I pressed up against the wall and began to bite my nails in frustration.

"To hell with this family," I hissed. "I'm better off on my own anyway.

Chapter 9

Three months later

My entire world had changed right before my very eyes. I gave up going to see Dr. Robinson because my life continued on a downward spiral, and I thought it was pointless. After being humiliated and thrown out of the house by my aunt, and then left on the streets by my mother, my life had become unpredictable. I found my way to a distant relative's house that day, and she let me stay with her for a few weeks. After that, the next three months were spent moving all across the city. I went from house to house with friends, friends of my extended family, and relatives on my father's side. Each house I moved into was seemingly worse than the previous one. I lived out of my bags and made the decision never to unpack because I knew it wouldn't be long before I was put out for some foolish reason. Some of the people I moved in with were mean and nasty. Some treated me like their personal slave to do their laundry and housework, while others turned me into a live-in babysitter for their children. I slept on couches, sofa beds, and sometimes the floor.

Finally, I decided to give my dad, Lewis, a call. Despite how my mom said he felt about me, I still loved him. His life was so unstable, and although he had never been there for me as a child, there was a special place in my heart for him. He was almost a millionaire. He had fame, fortune, and talent right at his fingertips and he lost it all within 365 days. He had been drafted into the NBA shortly after I was born. He also had a drug problem.

First, it was alcohol, and once he made it to the NBA, he began to use cocaine and heroin heavily. Those types of drugs were prevalent among NBA players during that time, so the association always did random drug tests. One day, he failed.

All of his talent, stardom, money, and everything he'd worked hard for was taken away from him, just like that. I always wanted to be a daddy's girl and to know just who he was.

There were times when my mother *would* allow me to call him. He would tell me he was on his way, and I would always get excited because that was my ticket away from my mother. Each time, I believed him. I sat by my window for days waiting for him, but he never showed up. I assumed one day he would.

The few times I *did* go to his house, he sent his girlfriend, Yvette, to pick me up. Yvette took care of him after his basketball years and before he was sent to prison.

She had a huge eight-bedroom home in the suburban part of Philadelphia. It was beautiful. I loved Yvette. My dad cheated on her with my mother and she got pregnant with me, but that didn't stop her from remaining in love with him. She took care of my dad and treated him like a king.

Yvette was the complete opposite of my mother. I wasn't her child, but she loved me as if I were. However, just like my dad's life was unstable, so were his women. I wasn't the only product of his infidelity.

My dad had gotten five other women pregnant while he was with Yvette.

Needless to say, I was surprised to find out that she was still there by his side when he got out of jail. They weren't a couple anymore, but she helped him out from time to time when he needed personal items, money, or in this case, housing his daughter.

Of all the places I had been to, I was happiest to move in with her. I knew all the hell I'd gone through was finally over. I walked up to her front door with my trash bag full of clothes and knocked on it. She opened the door with the biggest smile on her face.

"Hey baby," she greeted, instantly pulling me into her embrace.

I couldn't stop smiling.

"Come in." She gestured, stepping to the side. "I missed you girl. I was wondering where you were, and why I haven't heard from you. Are you *all right?*"

I walked into her home, placed my bag by the sofa, and closed the front door. "Yes, I'm okay. Just been moving a lot."

"Moving where?"

"All over. *Everywhere*—dozens of times in the last three months."

"Oh my goodness, I'm so sorry." Yvette looked as if she could cry. "I had no idea any of this was even happening."

"It's all right. I got used to it after a while. I'm happy to be here, though."

"And I'm happy to have you." She smiled. "Now, Lewis is supposed to pay me for your rent once a month, but knowing him, he'll never do it. I rent out my rooms here to tenants, so I can't put you in any of my bedrooms or I'll lose money, but I'm not going to put you on my living room couch either. You're family—you deserve better than that. I fixed up a space for you on the third floor."

She motioned for me to follow her up the two flights of stairs. I followed in anticipation. Finally, a real room with an actual bed. I didn't care what it looked like, I was just eager to have something that was mine.

"Here we are," she said cheerfully.

There was a very small room by the corner of one of the bathrooms. It was guarded by an old closet door, which she moved to the side, so we could get in. It was the boiler room. Inside the tiny, cramped space was a huge exposed water heater to the right, a cat litter box in the corner, one small window, and a dirty, ripped, cream-colored loveseat that reeked of cat spray.

You've got to be kidding me, I thought.

"It isn't much, but it's all I can offer you at the moment until your father comes up with your first month's rent. It's nice and warm in here, and Munchkin the kitten will keep you company. She loves people. I'll get you a blanket for the bed."

What bed? I don't see a bed, I thought. You couldn't fit half of a bed in there if you wanted to.

"Is the bed in another room?" I asked.

"No, it's right here," she said as she pointed to the filthy loveseat. "I have a big blanket to cover it, it'll feel like heaven once you lie down on it. I'll get it once I get back. I have to run a few errands. Be back shortly," she said and walked away.

"Oh, I almost forgot," she hollered from the hallway. "Could you help me out and clean up downstairs? I'm having dinner later on."

"Sure...no problem," I said with a counterfeit smile.

"Great. Thank you so much. I'm so glad you're here." She walked the few steps back to me, gave me a hug, and turned to leave.

I watched her disappear down the stairs and then turned back to my so-called room. My eyes began to fill with tears.

"The boiler room," I whispered quietly as my stomach turned. I was so disgusted, I wanted to spit.

Of all of the bedrooms in her big beautiful home, I was only worth a boiler room shared with an animal? *I thought I was worth more to Yvette than rent money. I guess times have changed.*

Shaking my head, I took a seat on the smelly loveseat and looked around the room at my reality. I swallowed, breathing heavily, unable to digest defeat. My mind became static as the horrors of the life I'd tried to forget began to replay in my mind. I was tired of moving, tired of living out of bags, and tired of being forced to accept the way people treated me. I didn't have a voice, I didn't have a real home, and the way it was looking, I wouldn't have a future either. My hands began to shake as I burst into tears.

An opened toolbox sat on the floor by the water heater. The first thing I noticed was a big utility blade sitting on top of the rest of the tools. Without thinking, I grabbed the blade and started to cut my forearm. I cut myself until the mental anguish I felt was drowned out by my physical pain. When I came out of it, I'd sliced my arm almost fifty times. It was swollen, bloody, burning, and throbbing with pain, but that pain could be fixed with a bandage and a Tylenol. It was much easier to deal with than the torment I suffered in my mind. At the age of sixteen, self-mutilation became my new way of coping and forgetting my problems.

Chapter 10

The next day I sat in fifth period psychology class bored out of my mind. It was warm outside, but I wore long sleeves to cover up my arms, which I had cut the night before. It still burned a little, but it was a constant reminder that my pain was real. I still couldn't believe the nerve of Yvette to give me that boiler room as a bedroom. I didn't want to stay there anymore, but I didn't have any place else to go. The bus ride to school was an hour and a half long, forcing me to get up by five every morning. I was tired, exhausted, and ready to get out of class. Mr. Singletary began a rant about the textbooks he was passing out.

"Welcome to the world of psychology," he passed out the last of the books.

"I had to pull a lot of strings to get us these books. The old ones were too beat up and ripped apart for anyone to read or study out of. I hope you guys like these."

The old books were better. Half of the pages in mine were ripped, so when we had to do homework, I never had to do all of it.

"Everyone turn to page sixteen," he instructed. "Today, we'll be discussing the difference between the brain and the mind."

I turned my pages to see what he was talking about. I never knew there was a difference between the two.

You could hear other students sighing in boredom in the background, but as I peered at my book, it was actually pretty interesting. My journal was on my desk and I was getting ready to pull it out to write, but I wanted to find out more about this psychology stuff. Nothing about school ever interested me so it was shocking when I realized I'd read the entire chapter of our textbook during class. I'd never known a thing about psychology, but this was interesting. I wanted to know more about the mind.

Mr. Singletary assigned us homework, and I couldn't wait to get home and do it, which was a first for me. The rest of my day was spent reading my psychology textbook in other classes. It talked about the different stages of development, proper parenting skills, and personality development. It also talked about depression. I remembered one of my classmates saying her brother had studied psychology in college, and I wondered if I could do the same thing.

The bell rang, signaling for school to be dismissed for the day. After gathering my things, I walked outside to meet Autumn. I spotted her as soon as I got out the door and I walked over to greet her.

"Hey cousin."

She turned around to greet me. "Hey girl." She smiled. "You ready?"

"Yeah." I nodded. "It sucks that we don't walk the same route anymore. I hate that I have to take all these buses."

"I know, me too. I'll still wait with you for your bus," she said as we started our walk to the bus stop. "So, how are things going with Yvette?"

Shrugging my shoulders, I replied, "It's okay, I guess. I mean, it's not heaven, but it's not as bad as the other places. It's all I have right now, so..."

"You know Aunt Carol has been telling the whole family what happened with you and Steve, and everyone believes her." Autumn rolled her eyes.

"I don't care what she says to people. You know I would never do anything like that," I assured her. "She knows I didn't do it either. She never wanted me there from the beginning, and neither did he. That was her way out."

"I know none of that stuff is true. You haven't even had a boyfriend yet," she said.

Thankfully, Autumn was on my side. It felt nice to have at least one blood relative who believed me.

The bus pulled alongside the curb in front of me.

"All right." She leaned in and hugged me. "See you tomorrow. Call me when you get in."

"Okay cool." I stepped up on the bus and walked to the back to take my seat.

It was a shame what my family thought of me. Sometimes I wished I wasn't related to any of them.

There had to be another way out. *Once I graduate high school, then what?* I sat back in my seat, peering out the large window. *What will become of me once I turn eighteen?*

Soon, living with people would cost me money that I didn't have. I was tired of having my life placed in the hands of people who didn't care about it. There had to be some sort of future within me. I could either go to college or sell drugs on the street for a living.

My mood brightened up a bit as I chuckled to myself at the thought of selling drugs as a form of survival. Even though I was a bit disruptive, one thing was for sure: I wasn't built for the streets.

College was my best bet. I could get an education, start a career, and build my own empire. Reaching into my schoolbag, I pulled out my psychology textbook and stared down at it. It was the middle of my 11th grade year and I only had a 1.3 GPA. My report cards are always full of Fs and Ds, especially since my home life had been so unstable the past few months. Could I really make a turnaround within a year? Surely, I owed it to myself to try.

Chapter 11

Later that evening, I sat at Yvette's dining room table as she prepared dinner. One of her long-time girlfriends, Eve, had just walked in and greeted us. I remembered Eve from when I was younger. She was an annoying freeloader who always came next door to Yvette's to eat her food and gossip.

"Hey Eve." Yvette turned her back to open the fridge.

"Hey there. Do you know your lights are still on in your car?"

"Oh no. Mystery, go cut those lights off, will you?" Yvette reached into her pocket for her keys and threw them to me.

"*Mystery*?" Eve's mouth dropped open and Yvette laughed as I stood up to get her keys. "Lewis's daughter?" She looked at me in a state of shock.

"Yes, that's her," Yvette said. "Missy, you remember Eve, don't you?"

"Yes, I remember. Hello," I said dryly, walking out the front door. I couldn't stand her. She was about to say something ignorant about my weight and my appearance, I just knew it. That was always the first thing out of the mouth of anybody who hadn't seen me in a while. I walked to Yvette's car and cut off her lights. As I made my back into the house, the front door swung open and Eve stepped out of it, pointing at me.

"Yvette, that is *not* that pretty little girl of Lewis's. You've got to be kidding me. She got so fat." Her voice was overly loud and obnoxious.

"That's her." Yvette laughed in the background. "And lower your voice please. You're always so over the top."

I walked past Eve and back into the house. Her eyes followed me the entire time.

"Oh my God, I haven't seen you since you were a little girl. How old are you now?" she asked.

"I'm sixteen." I sat back down at the dinner table.

"Sixteen? Jesus, girl, you look twenty-five. You need to slow down on all that eating."

There it is. I'd known it was only a matter of time.

"You were the most beautiful little chocolate girl I'd ever laid eyes on. I used to try to dress my daughters the way your mother dressed you. I can't *believe* what I'm looking at." She sat down at the table next to me.

"What happened to all your beautiful hair? Where's your mother?" Eve asked.

"Eve, will you *shut up* and get out of that child's business." Yvette laughed again as she carried the food over to the table.

"I'll be back." I got up from the table and headed up the stairs.

"I wasn't trying to be mean. It's just shocking to see her again. She looks like a little tomboy. Is she gay?" I heard Eve ask.

"I don't think so. I've never seen her with any boys though," Yvette responded.

I continued up the stairs, moving as fast as I could to escape their annoying voices. I barged into the bathroom, fighting back the tears I wanted to let fall from my eyes.

Disgusted, I stared down at myself. This felt like Deja vu all over again. When my mother could no longer afford to send me to private school, she put me in public school. Before school began in September, she took me shopping and bought me a pair of jeans and two shirts, one long-sleeved and one short-sleeved. She told me that because of my weight clothes in my size were too expensive. She promised she'd never buy me any more until I lost weight. She told me the kids at school would call me dirty for wearing the same clothes every day. She said maybe if they teased me and picked on me enough, I would lose weight. And they did. They picked on me during the day and chased me home after school. And my mom loved every bit of it. Lifting up my shirt, I took a good look at my overweight self in the mirror. I looked down at my flabby stomach, and then I stretched my arms out and cringed at the fat hanging down from them.

I was tired of being teased, but I had no clue how to control my weight. After being starved as a child, I'd never had a healthy relationship with food. The day I moved out of my mother's reach, I scarfed down food like it was the last supper, and now, I wasn't pretty anymore. At least, not to society's standards. I sure did miss the days when people would stop and stare at my beauty. I missed the applause and the validation. I missed the accolades, because that meant "I love you". I wanted to be loved. Maybe if I lost weight, people would love me like that again.

Looking at the toilet, the only thing that came to mind was getting all the food I had eaten out of me. I didn't know how to diet, but I did know how to throw up. Without thinking, I dropped to my knees in front of the toilet bowl and forced myself to vomit. *Hello, Bulimia.*

Chapter 12

Six months later

Senior year had come much faster than I expected, but it was certainly welcomed with open arms. There were only five months left in the school year, and I would be a high school graduate. I spent the remainder of 11th grade in my schoolbooks, especially psychology. I was on a mission to get the hell out of Philly and used all my time after school to go to the library and study. I did packet upon packet of makeup work to bring my grades up. I even did summer school classes for extra credit. I started junior year with Ds and Fs and finished with Bs and Cs.

My weight had dropped significantly over the past six months as well. I threw up every bit of food I ate. Despite the constant hunger pains and dizzy spells, people weren't focused on how fat I was anymore. Fifty pounds of weight loss had made a huge difference. Finally, I felt like I fit in with the rest of the world...physically, at least.

My dad had come back to live with Yvette, and he managed to get a job at a local sneaker store to help her out with bills. When the money came in, she had no problem putting me in a more comfortable room in the house.

Yvette also started taking me to the hairdresser with her every two weeks, and she helped me build a new wardrobe. She made me get rid of the boyish clothing and got me clothes that actually fit. For once in my life, things seemed to be trending in my favor.

One particular Tuesday afternoon, we had lunch at Red Lobster. I'd stayed home from school because I'd slept through my alarm and missed the bus. Yvette got off work early and decided to take me to look at prom dresses, so I met her in town.

"How was the food?" She pulled out her credit card to pay the bill.

"It was great," I replied.

"Your dad's going to be mad he missed out," she squealed. "He loves the food here."

"I did tell him before I left that we were probably going to lunch after shopping, but he said he had something to do."

"Yeah right." She rolled her eyes. "He doesn't have a *thing* to do. He needs to be out looking for another job.

"Well as long as you keep handicapping him, he'll never get one."

"This is true," she agreed with a head nod as the waiter came by and took her credit card.

"I'll meet you at the car." I stood from my seat. "I have to use the bathroom."

"Okay," she muttered.

Grabbing my purse from the table, I hurried toward the back of the restaurant where the restroom was located and thanked God I was the only one in there. I went into the stall, shoved my fingers down my throat, and began to vomit. My life had become secret trips to the bathroom and razor blades stuffed in my socks. I knew I had a problem, but at the moment, it didn't faze me as much as it should've. It was dangerous and unhealthy, but I was in too deep to let up now.

When I finished unloading my stomach, I cleaned myself up at the sink, wiped my face, headed out of the bathroom and to the car.

Yvette pulled out of the parking lot and began the fifteen-minute drive back to our house.

"Tell me again what your guidance counselor told you about financial aid for college?" she asked.

"She said I needed to fill out the paperwork. It's some kind of form that requires my parent's income and needs to be sent in to see how much money I'm eligible for. My mother would never fill that out, and Dad gets paid under the table."

"I can't fill it out for you—I'm not your legal guardian." Yvette shook her head, feeling bad that she couldn't help. "You've been doing so well academically since last year, too. Have you applied to any colleges yet?"

"No, not yet. The librarian gave me some applications. I was going to fill them out the other day in the library, until I found about the financial aid stuff."

"So, the college idea just went out the window?"

"No, not completely. I just need to figure out some more stuff, that's all."

"I'm sorry I can't help, but I can help with the fun stuff, like prom." Her eyes lit up. "Speaking of that... are you excited? You've lost all that weight and have a nice little curvy body now. I know you're ready to show off your new figure."

"Not really." I laughed. "I don't have a date...I really don't even want to go."

"Why not?"

"Because prom is overrated and too expensive. I'm just trying to graduate and get it over with."

The truth was, I did want to go, but my arms were covered in razor scars. I kept them hidden under long sleeve shirts. No one knew about my bad habits.

"You should. Your father has missed out on your entire life. It would be nice for him to see you off on your prom," she said.

"I guess..." I smiled then changed the subject. "You're happy he's back, aren't you?"

"For now, until he gets caught doing something else and then I'll put him out again." Yvette laughed.

"He seems different this time. I think he's changed for good. He's home all the time and doesn't appear to be using drugs anymore."

"Let's hope he's changed." Yvette pulled up to our house.

"Hey, isn't that Eve's car?" I pointed to the car that was parked on the street next to our driveway.

"Looks like it," Yvette answered with a confused look on her face. "She just called me before I left work asking what I was doing because she was on her way to the hairdresser."

Yvette got out of the car and started up the driveway. I got out and followed behind her. In my head, I drew my own conclusion as to what we were about to walk into when Yvette opened that door. My dad was so scandalous—so much for being a changed man. As we neared the door, you could hear kitchen items rattling and my dad's baritone voice moaning in delight.

Yvette's face turned bright red as her mouth dropped open. "You've got to be *kidding* me."

She reached into her purse and pulled out her pistol. As soon as I saw it, my eyes widened.

"Everything I've done for that *bitch*," she spat as her four-inch stilettos clicked loudly up the concrete.

"Yvette, don't do anything stupid with that gun, please," I cried, trotting behind her, afraid of what was about to happen.

"Missy, go back to the car," she hissed.

"No, I will not. We *both* need to go back to the car. My dad is in there and you have a loaded gun."

"I told that fool he had one more time to cheat on me and that was it." Yvette cocked her pistol, put her hand on the trigger, and walked up the steps. "And *this* is it!"

"Yvette, wait a minute." I tried to catch up to her, but it was too late. She pushed the door open wildly.

"Think about what you—"

We both stopped dead in our tracks as soon as we saw my dad. He was pressed against the kitchen counter having sex, but it wasn't with Eve—it was with Eve's husband.

"Oh my God!" I yelled.

My dad and Eve's husband, James, both gasped when they saw us. James quickly grabbed himself in shame.

"What the *hell*!" Yvette shrieked.

"Yvette." My dad grabbed his underwear. "I can explain."

"Lewis, you told me she was working," James hissed at my dad.

Yvette's eyes were stone cold. She loved my dad, despite everything he had put her through. No matter how often they broke up, when someone spoke his name, you could still see that fire of passion for him burning in her eyes.

This time, though, the fire was put out. She glared at my dad, her blood running cold, and before anyone could take another breath, she started shooting in his direction.

"In my *house*, Lewis?" she screamed as she continued to shoot mercilessly. James and Lewis both dodged out of the way and ran for the door. James ran out the back door of the kitchen, and my dad ducked to the ground and scurried out the front door.

Yvette turned around toward the door where I was standing and pointed the gun. I turned around and ducked, clutching my purse, following behind my dad as she pulled the trigger and bullets began to fly.

"Yvette," I screamed, "Stop!"

"I'm done," she yelled as she stopped shooting and threw her gun inside the house. "Only because your daughter is out there with you, you *sick* son of a bitch."

My dad continued down the driveway and stopped behind Yvette's car. He had nowhere to go, and no car keys. I didn't either.

"Yvette, calm down," I pleaded.

"Did you know about this?" She squinted her eyes at me.

"What? No," I said defensively. "I—"

"To hell with that," she snapped. "I don't trust either one of you. *Both* of you get off my driveway."

"Where am I going to go? I didn't have anything to do with—"

"You and your faggot father get *off* my property before I empty this clip into both of you."

"Come on Mystery," my dad whispered to me, "before she kills us both."

"No," I hissed. "I don't want to go anywhere with *you*." Disappointment coated my tone.

"You have five seconds to get *off* my property." Yvette began to count down before heading back into her house to grab her gun.

"Do you really have a choice?" my dad asked. "*Let's go.*"

He moved away from Yvette's car and ran around the corner. He had no shirt on, and his underwear was on backward. As Yvette continued to countdown, I realized she was serious. By the time she got to two, she pulled her trigger. I looked up at her, and she stared back at me, heartless. I knew it was time for me to go. I moved away from her car and ran down the street, following my dad.

Here we go again, I thought. *Another dead end.*

My dad ran around the corner into Eve's house with James, but I stopped in my tracks when he ran up the stairs. I didn't want to go in there. I still couldn't believe what I had just witnessed, and it was extremely awkward. Somehow, my parents always found a way to ruin things for me.

Crossing the street, I walked over to a nearby park and sat behind the empty baseball diamond. My life was so unpredictable, always going from one extreme to the next without warning. There I was again, homeless. Opening my purse, I pulled out my razor blade.

Chapter 13

With each cut, I thought about my dreams, my goals, and my future—all headed down the drain. I was going to be stuck in this cycle *forever*. I'd never get ahead in life. My mother had been right: I'd lost. She'd won. She said I would never be anything, Aunt Carol told me I would never be anything, and they were right. Every path I took to better myself landed me at a dead end. Every home I moved into was worse than the one before it. Nothing in my life was ever consistent, and it felt like it never would be.

As I finished my cutting episode, I placed my blade back into my purse. My arms stung like crazy and dripped with blood, but my pain validated exactly how I felt. Using a tissue from my purse, I wiped my arms, pulled my sleeves down, and continued to sit behind the baseball field. I had begun to reflect on what had just taken place when suddenly, a soft voice emerged from behind me.

"Are you okay?"

I turned to see who it was, and it was a random girl. I knew she went to my school because she had on the gym uniform, but I had never seen her before.

"I'm fine." I quickly wiped my tears and stood up. The girl proceeded to walk toward me.

"Are you sure?" she asked. "Because I think I just saw you cutting yourself."

My eyes got big and I was filled with embarrassment at the thought of someone watching me without my permission.

"You didn't see anything," I shot back angrily. "Mind your own business."

She continued walking toward me, paying no mind to my attitude. "I've seen you around before. Aren't you related to Autumn?"

"Yeah. She's my cousin," I replied.

"Okay, yeah." She smiled. "She goes to my church. I think I've seen you there a few times as well. Do you go to Overbrook High School, too?"

"Why?" I asked defensively.

"Because I want to know, that's all."

Every Sunday, Autumn attended a storefront Pentecostal church in southwest Philadelphia. Sometimes I went with her. The last church I ever attended as a member was with my mother and grandmother, but since being disconnected from them, I stopped going. Autumn loved church, and when I lived with Aunt Carol, I would go with her on Sundays to get away from home. The people there were nice, and the church was very welcoming.

This girl didn't look familiar to me at all, but then again, I didn't pay attention to anyone when I went.

"Yeah, I go to Overbrook." I stood up to walk out of the park in an attempt to get away from the girl.

"What grade are you in?" She continued to follow me.

"Why? Why you asking me so many questions? Are you trying to spy on me for Yvette or something?"

Because if so, like I told her, I knew *nothing* about this."

The girl looked very confused. "No. I go to Overbrook as well. I left school early because I had a doctor's appointment. I live up the street, and I usually come here to read my bible after school. You're actually sitting in my spot."

"The bible?" I replied. "You actually *read* it?"

She giggled. "Of course."

"Why?"

"It's my way of hearing from God," she said.

I couldn't help but laugh. "And you talk to him, I suppose?"

"I sure do," she replied confidently.

"And what does he tell you?"

"Well, for starters, he led me to talk to you. He put me right here, at this very moment, to notice what you were doing. I'm not judging you, and I don't think you're some kind of freak. I don't know you, but I was genuinely concerned."

I stopped walking and looked at her. She seemed so innocent and sweet. Instantly, I felt horrible for fussing and laughing at her.

"I'm Sugar," she said sweetly, extending her hand out for me to shake.

"*Sugar?*" I raised my eyebrows. "I'm not calling another woman Sugar unless that's your real name."

"That *is* my real name." She smiled. "What's yours?"

"Spice." I chuckled as we began our walk back toward the school.

"Very funny."

"I'm Missy."

"Oh, that's cute. What's it short for?"

"Mystery."

"That's different, very unique, and pretty." She smiled.

"I hate it. Both my parents were light skinned, and I came out chocolate and didn't look like either of them, so my mom named me Mystery."

"Well my mom said when I came out, I had the face of an angel. I came out smiling, full of life, and ready for the world so she named me Sugar, the sweetest thing on earth." She giggled.

Her name was pretty cool, actually. As my defenses began to die down, I was able to get a good look at Sugar. She was absolutely beautiful. She had mocha-colored skin, and her hair was individually braided with hair extensions that went down her back. She was about five feet, five inches tall, and looked to be about a size five. She had a beautiful smile and perfect teeth. I had never seen her in school before—nothing sweet ever came out of Overbrook. I always kept to myself, however, so it was possible I could've overlooked her.

"How long have you been here, and what grade are you in?" I asked.

"I'm in 11th," she replied. "Been here since freshman year."

"Oh cool. I've never seen you around before."

"I've seen you plenty of times, and always wanted to stop and say hi, but you never looked approachable. You always look mean. I stay away from people like that." She laughed.

"I'm not mean...I'm just not into trusting everybody these days. My main focus has been trying to get my grades up, so I can go to college next year."

"That's awesome. Which one?"

"I don't know." I shrugged. "I just know I want to go, and my grades have been horrible since freshman year. I found out this morning that I might not be able to go, though. I haven't filled out any applications and there's some kind of financial aid form I didn't know about, and they need my parents' information."

"Are you unable to get that information?"

"I don't know where they are," I admitted. "Well...I do know where my dad is, but he doesn't have any financial information."

"And your mom?"

"I know where she is too."

"But?"

There was no way I was going to tell this girl all my business; I'd just met her. "It's a long story. Everything is just a mess. I was really looking forward to college. What about you? Are you interested in college?" I asked to get the conversation off of me.

"I don't know." She shrugged. "I'm not sure what I want to do yet. I like doing hair, so maybe I'll go to cosmetology school, or if I do decide to go to a college, it'll be a community one here in the city. That way I'll be close to church and my sister."

"You like church a lot, huh?"

"I do." Her eyes lit up. "You should come visit again, I think you'd enjoy it, too."

"I enjoyed it when I came a few times with my cousin. Maybe I'll come back soon. I'll think about it."

"Okay, well, I'm going to head home. Let's exchange numbers. We should hang out." Sugar pulled out her cellphone.

"Okay." I reached for mine as well. Yvette paid my cellphone bill, but I wasn't sure how much longer it would be on after today.

"Have you prayed about college?" she asked me.

"No. God doesn't care anything about me," I said. "I believe he's real and everything, but he doesn't exist in *my* life, trust me."

"Are you saved?"

"Listen, I was brought up in church—I know everything about it. I'm not new to being a Christian, but me and God aren't the best of friends. I mean, if we were, I don't think he would've let me—" I paused. I wasn't going to let myself travel down memory lane when the path wasn't worth the trip. I just shook my head. "Never mind. I'll talk to you later, Sugar. It was nice meeting you."

Just as I turned to walk away, Sugar grabbed my arm. "Everything happens for a reason, Missy. Sometimes we may not understand it. Heck, we may not even like it, but nothing in life ever happens by coincidence or chance. It happens because God allows it. It doesn't always feel good, but in the end, it works out for your good. If you really want to go to school, apply...*today*. If you've never had faith in God before, try it now. Tell him what you want and have faith that if it's in his will, he will make it happen, money or no money."

The way she talked about God at such a young age began to warm my heart. I'd never met someone so young who was so certain and sure about God.

"I'll try," I said, "but I need more than just a prayer...I need a miracle."

"God has the power to open doors twenty-four hours a day. Paul and Silas are reminders that doors can still open at midnight." Smiling, she turned on her feet and walked away.

I didn't know who Paul or Silas were, but the way this girl talked gave me hope.

My mind contemplated her advice as I sat back down behind the baseball diamond. Sugar was right—the least I could do was just apply. *The worst thing they can do is reject me, right?*

It took the kind words of a stranger to give me the push I needed. My eyes traveled to the sleeve that hid my hideous imperfections. It was almost as if I could see right through the material. A burning sensation still lingered on the area of my newest affliction.

Taking a deep breath, I slowly opened my mouth and tried something new for the first time.

"God, I know we don't talk often, but I know you're real. I believe in you, but I'm not so sure that the feeling is mutual. I don't know why you've allowed me to suffer so much. Did I do something wrong? Did I disappoint you, too, with my looks at birth? Did I cry too much as a baby? Was I too big? Too tall? Too mouthy? If I ever did anything to hurt you, I'm sorry. I really want to get away from these people here. I'm trying my best, but it doesn't seem to be good enough at this point, so I need your help. You know my situation, you've watched me go through it. I don't have anyone but you right now, and I need you. Please help me. In Jesus' name, amen."

The first college application I remembered receiving from my guidance counselor was for Shippensburg University. Immediately, I pulled out my phone and Googled the president of the university. I had a gut feeling that I should reach out to her. If I was going to explain my situation to anyone, it was going to be her. Submitting my application without a financial aid form was definitely not going to get her attention. Hopefully, my letter would.

Chapter 14

A week had passed since the incident with my dad. When Eve found out what happened with her husband, she left him and moved in with her mother on the other side of town. My dad didn't have any place to go, so he moved in with James. I didn't have any place else to go either, so I had no choice but to stay with the two of them. I never questioned my dad about his sexuality. Honestly, I didn't care. He was a wreck, and so was James. He began to use drugs again, and James followed suit. They used James's money and would leave for days at a time to go on drug binges. It was fine by me because I didn't want to be around them anyway.

I hung out with Sugar every day. We started meeting at the baseball diamond to hang around and talk. She gave off so much positivity about life and God. I really enjoyed being around her. I wanted to learn more about just who God was and what he was capable of doing, so I began to attend church with Sugar. That same day I met her, actually, I texted her asking when she'd be going to church next, and she told me she would be going to bible study that night. Her pastor came to get us, and I was hooked. That Sunday, I joined. One Friday night, her grandmother cooked dinner, and even though I tried not to eat, I didn't want to be rude. Afterward, we sat out on her steps.

"So, are you ever going to invite me into your house?" she asked.

"It's not my house," I told her. "Besides, you wouldn't want to see what was in there."

"Why not?"

"Because you wouldn't."

"Your guard is always up, and it's so unnecessary with me. I don't want to do anything but be your friend." She laughed.

"It's a habit, sorry." I got up from the step, "I'll be right back. I have to run to my house really quick."

"It's late, I'll walk with you." Sugar got up.

"*No*. No need. I'm just going to the bathroom, I won't be long."

"Why can't you just use my bathroom?"

I really needed throw up and didn't want to risk anyone hearing me at Sugar's house, but she was too persistent and always up under me.

"Okay fine. I'll use your bathroom." I turned around and walked back.

"It's upstairs to the right," she said.

"Thanks. You don't need to walk me." I laughed. "I'll be able to find it."

"I wasn't planning on it, smarty." Sugar rolled her eyes.

I went upstairs into her bathroom and threw up my dinner. When I was finished, I was so dizzy, but I shook it off. For a brief moment, I leaned on the sink to get my head together. My headaches were coming even more frequently. All the throwing up and lost nutrients was beginning to take a toll on me. After a few splashes of water on my face, I went back downstairs to sit with Sugar.

"You know, this whole week has got me on cloud nine," I admitted, sitting down beside her.

"How come?"

"I don't know...just being involved and committed to learning about God. It kind of gives me peace in my hopeless situation."

"Yeah, I feel you. I was like that when I first started going."

"I feel good about all of this." I nodded. "Our talks and church are the only consistency in my life right now."

"Oh yeah?" she said. "Well, I'm glad I can help."

Whenever the doors were open, I was there. Autumn didn't go to church as much anymore. I barely even hung out with her lately.

Having a new church family was a blessing. I had finally made my first friend that wasn't blood-related. Over the next few weeks, Sugar and I became so close, so quickly. It was the first time I'd ever connected with anyone, and it felt good. We had a lot in common, but most importantly, she kept me motivated.

We laughed and joked on her steps until it was time for me to go home. She and her sister, Casey, walked me halfway. When I got home, I called to let her know I was in, and we ended up talking on the phone half of the night.

Chapter 15

One month later

"I was thinking about cutting my hair." Sugar examined herself in the mirror. "What do you think? I could pull off an Amber Rose, right?"

I looked up in her direction from my spot on her bed. "Better you than me." I laughed just as I felt my phone vibrating.

Yvette's name flashed on my screen, and my eyes instantly widened in shock. *Why is she calling me?* I thought. The first time, I didn't answer, but she called back...twice.

I reached for my phone and answered on the fifth ring. "Hello?"

"Hey Missy, how are you?"

How am I? I'm just fine—you're the one that needs to be answering that question.

"Good," I replied.

"Listen, I'm not going to hold you. You have mail here from Shippensburg University," she told me. "It looks important."

My heart nearly stopped.

"Oh my God."

"What happened?" Sugar turned to me and asked.

"I'll be right there." I quickly ended the call.

"Who was that?" Sugar approached me.

"My dad's ex-girlfriend."

"The crazy shooter?"

"Yup, she just told me a letter came from one of the colleges I applied to," I said eagerly.

Sugar shared my excitement. "Oh my God! I'm coming with you."

"I don't know what you'll are talking about, but I'm coming too!" Casey, her thirteen-year-old sister, said when she entered the room.

"This is the moment I've been waiting for, and I'm terrified."

The three of us hurried out of the house and began to walk the six blocks toward Yvette's. We walked as fast as we could. Halfway there, I got lightheaded.

"Hang on," I said in between deep breaths. "I can't walk that fast."

"You all right?" Casey asked.

"I'm fine, just a little dizzy. Let's just slow down a bit."

"You *sure* you're okay?" Sugar looked at me as if she was trying to read my mind. "You *have* been a bit sluggish lately."

"Yes," I snapped back. "Can we just change the subject?"

I hated when people asked me questions after I responded to them, especially when I was lying about something.

"Fine." Sugar rolled her eyes. "With your nasty attitude—"

"Both of you *shut up*," Casey interjected. "It's not that serious."

"She's going to regret talking to me like that when she gets into college and realizes I'm not there. She'll miss me." Sugar laughed.

"No, I won't, because you and Case are going to come visit every chance you get. That's if they even accepted me. They probably wrote me back saying, *Sorry, we don't accept excuses. No financial aid, no acceptance."*

"No. I believe God. There is more out there for you, and Philly can't offer it. You belong in a college. You made it this far.

"Me too," Casey agreed. "And I'm excited to be a part of it. You're going to be somebody one day— hopefully somebody with some money so you can pay me back for all the change you keep stealing out of my piggy bank to buy water ice and shit."

"Casey, watch your mouth." Sugar reached out to push her. Casey dodged it and ran up the street.

I loved both of them. I hated being in Philadelphia my entire life. College would be my golden ticket out of there, but all of a sudden, it hit me: if I was accepted, I'd have to leave them. I never thought I'd have mixed, bittersweet feelings about leaving Philadelphia. Having a friend I connected with, and having her little sister look up to me made me feel good. A void in my life had finally been filled.

As we approached Yvette's steps, I could see a large white piece of mail sitting face up in the black mailbox.

I was glad she'd left it in the mailbox for me. I really didn't want to see her, and I supposed the feeling was mutual.

My heart began to beat like a drum. *This is it.* I walked up the steps and stood at the mailbox, staring at the letter. Casey and Sugar finally made it up the steps as well.

"That's it right there?" Casey asked.

"Yeah," I said nervously.

"Well pick it up."

"I know, stop torturing yourself," Sugar added. She reached in the mailbox and grabbed the letter. "Open it."

She handed me the envelope. Ripping it open as fast as I could, I stared at the letter in disbelief as I read the first line. I looked it over about three times to make sure I wasn't seeing things.

"I got in," I screamed. "Oh my goodness. They told me to just come. I was offered a full scholarship."

Sugar gasped in shock. Casey hugged me tightly then proceeded to do a celebration dance on the steps.

"See, I told you," Sugar smiled.

I just stood there looking at the letter. I couldn't believe my eyes. Nothing had *ever* worked out in my favor until this point. I must have read my acceptance letter about a hundred times.

Dear Mystery Johnson,

Congratulations. It is my pleasure to inform you of your acceptance to Shippensburg University.

Chapter 16

After receiving my acceptance to Shippensburg University, life began to get better. The rest of my time in high school flew by. Graduation came and went. My grandmother paid for everything and made sure I had everything I needed. Both sets of my grandparents came, and one of my aunts. Sugar and Casey were there, and so was their mother.

That entire summer, I had a *blast*. I fell in love with my church and participated in everything possible: praise dance, youth choir, adult choir— you name it, I did it. I was there for Sunday school, worship service, and afternoon services. On Wednesdays I was in bible study, and on the weekends my pastor usually had something going on for the youth. The church practically became my home. Sugar and I both worked at the church's summer camp and had a blast.

It was my last night in town before leaving for school. Sugar and I were walking back to her grandmother's house from the water ice stand, eating our ice cream, when I received a text message from my Aunt Carol.

Hi baby, this is Aunt Carol. Just wanted to tell you I'm so proud of you and your success. I'm so glad God put me in your life to help catapult you into being the beautiful young lady you are today. Tough love still works. Let me know what you need for school and I will get it for you.

I looked at my phone in utter disbelief. "She has *some* nerve."

"Who does?" Sugar asked.

"My Aunt Carol," I replied. "She just texted me. Remember the one who threw me out of the house in a bath towel?"

"Yeah..." Sugar nodded. "She still with that guy?"

"Who knows?"

"What'd she say?"

Turning my phone to Sugar, I showed her the message. "It's funny how people use tough love as an excuse to disrespect, mistreat, and use you. I really can't believe her. I don't even know what to say in response to that," I said.

"Don't say anything. Pastor always says many create a need to respond, but few create a *desire* to respond. Pick your battles."

"You're right."

"I can't believe your aunt did all that stuff to you. What ever happened to your mom?" Sugar asked.

"She lives in Arizona now," I replied. "I haven't seen her since the day she dropped me off in the street half naked. I was hurt a lot growing up. We talked about a lot of things, but there is still so much I haven't shared with you."

Sugar shook her head. With her, I felt as though I could tell her anything. I'd debated in my mind whether or not to shine a light on my demons. I wanted her to know. She'd helped me so much until that point; maybe sharing that part of me with her would help me stop.

"I've been made fun of a lot because of my weight," I continued, "treated like a loner by every caregiver I've had. I started cutting myself last year to try to make sense of the pain, and I became bulimic shortly after that in an attempt to control my weight. There have been times when I considered killing myself or running far, far away from here because I felt alone. At the end of the day, I don't have a real home or real genuine love. I did see a counselor for a short while, and she encouraged me to further my education. That's part of why I started to take school seriously. Other than college, I don't have a future to look forward to."

A brief silence lingered between us. Sugar looked ahead as if she were in deep thought.

"Everything makes sense to me now," she said. "I'm *so* glad you have me. Forget those people—all the ones who laughed at you, gave up on you, and dismissed you are going to be so amazed by what God's going to do for you. He always saves the best for last."

We approached her grandmother's house and sat down on the steps.

"So what about you? How come you live with your grandmother?"

"My parents were married for over twenty years. My dad has a crazy temper. He used to beat on my mom. She left him...and then left us."

I was shocked to hear that come out of her mouth. I supposed there were things she didn't share with me either.

"Did...did he ever beat you?" I asked hesitantly.

Sugar slowly nodded her head. "Yes. Case, too. My grandmother took us in when she found out," she finished.

"Where is your dad now?"

"He's around. He doesn't live too far from here, but he doesn't come to see us."

"Did you ever expect life to turn out like this?" I asked her.

"No, not at all, but God does everything for a reason. If I didn't know him, I'd probably have gone crazy by now."

"Well, I'm glad we have each other. Even though I'll be two hours away, I'm still here for you."

"I know." She smiled. "I can't wait to come up there to see you."

"Yeah, so we can prank everyone, and you have to send me pictures and videos of church stuff. I want to know everything Pastor talks about on Sundays and Wednesdays."

"Yeah I will," Sugar said. "I just can't believe you're leaving. Summer came and went so fast. I'm going to miss you. Casey will too—she loves you."

"I know. I'll be home in December for Christmas vacation for about a month, and we'll be back to our old selves."

"Yeah," she responded with a somber glow.

My eyes got teary as a gush of emotion hit me. I wiped them away just as my grandmother's jeep pulled up in front of us.

"You ready?" she shouted out of her window. "You still have packing to do for tomorrow."

"Here I come," I shouted as I stood up from the steps, giving Sugar the biggest hug.

"Tell Casey I tried to wait around to say goodbye, but she took too long." I began to walk toward my grandmother's car.

"I will," Sugar said. She was on the verge of crying herself. "Have fun, Missy. Call me when you get in."

"Okay." I got into my grandmother's car and closed the door.

As we pulled off, I watched Sugar wipe a tear from her cheek and look in another direction, so I couldn't see her face. Tears began to fall from my own face. She was an angel in disguise, and probably one of the best things that had ever happened to me. I was really going to miss my friend.

Chapter 17

My grandparents drove me to Shippensburg University around eight the next morning. It was a three-hour drive. I was extremely exhausted by the time we pulled up, but as soon as I saw the school's sign, all I could do was smile. There was a whole world of endless possibilities getting ready to open up for me, and I couldn't wait.

After we unloaded the truck, my grandparents said their goodbyes and got back on the road. As I looked around my dorm, I thought I was in paradise. For the first time in four years, I had my own room. I had a closet, a desk, and a dresser. I didn't have pictures, decorations, or a lot of clothes to unpack, but the things I did have that had been bought for me were greatly appreciated. When you have nothing, anything seems like something.

Shortly after, I met my roommate. She came in with her mother, father, and loads of boxes and bags.

"Hey," she greeted. "I'm Jazmin."

"I'm Missy." I smiled.

Her parents waved to me with big smiles as I sat on my bed and texted Sugar while Jazmin and her family unpacked.

A few times, my eyes wandered over to Jazmin and her mother. They laughed and conversed while hanging pictures and putting away her clothes. Her father set up her gigantic television and continued to bring up her equipment. When it was time for them to leave, they showered her with hugs and kisses. They told her how proud they were of her, and how they couldn't wait to see her during the first winter break. They wished her good luck, gave her money, and left.

"That's a lot of stuff you have," I said.

It looked like she'd brought her whole house with her.

"I didn't know what all you had, so I just brought everything." She laughed. "What's mine is yours. Feel free to help yourself to anything."

Her mother came back into the room.

"Come here Jaz," she said. "I need another hug before I go. I can't just up and leave." Her mother grabbed her and embraced her. "I can't believe this day is really here. I'm so proud of you."

As much as I was excited for my new journey into college, seeing that left me feeling bittersweet. I walked out of my room and onto the beautiful crowded college campus full of families there for move-in day. I found myself surrounded by the very thing I'd run all the way there to escape. I yearned for love, affection, relationships, and acceptance from people who cared. Yet again, I was forced to watch those things being given to everyone but me. I was in the middle of an important milestone in my life, forced to go through it alone and mentally suffer by watching everyone around me enjoy what I wanted.

*****

My first semester of college seemed to go by so quickly. It was already December, and I had already met so many wonderful people. I excelled academically, especially in psychology. I even started to develop a career plan in the field for when I graduated.

Everything from student programs to social events—I was there. I used my refund check to pay for driving classes, and once I obtained my driver's license, I was able to buy my first car. It was hardly anything fancy, but it was mine. I was able to get a part-time job on campus not too far from my dorm.

And then there was Brian. I met him during freshman week. Come to find out, he was also from Philly and knew Sugar. Brian went to the church she used to go to with her grandmother, and needless to say, she egged on us, encouraging us to get close.

It was the week of finals, and I was headed back to campus after my work shift was over. My car had been running on fumes, so I stopped by the local gas station. When I pulled up, it was extremely crowded. All the pumps were taken, so I had to sit behind two cars to wait my turn. I pulled out my phone and began to text Sugar. I loved my best friend. We had become so close. Even with me going off to college, we texted and talked day and night. Every time something good or bad happened to either of us, we were on our phones gossiping about it. That was my girl, my best friend. I didn't know how I'd ever get by without her.

After about fifteen minutes of waiting, the last car finally pulled away. As I put my car in drive to pull up to the gas pump, another car came barging in front of me and got to the pump before I could. It happened so quickly, I had to slam on my brakes to keep from ramming into them.

"What the hell?" I put my phone down and got out of my car.

It was a girl who went to my school, one of my roommate's cocky, arrogant, thinks-she's-better-than-everybody friends.

"Hello?" I approached her. "You just cut in front of me. I've been sitting here for twenty minutes. I *know* you saw my car here."

"Well, you were on your phone and took too long to move. I'm late for work. You'll be all right, I won't be long," she replied with a snotty attitude as she unscrewed her gas cap.

Another girl sitting in the car next to her began to laugh hysterically. "What's wrong with you, Kelly? Stop being such a bully."

"*Kelly's* losing her damn mind, that's what wrong with her," I responded angrily as I felt my temper begin to flare up.

I'd spent my entire life being treated unfairly by everyone, and I *never* had any control over it. Now that I had an opinion and a voice, I wasn't about to have anyone treat me like dirt anymore. A mixture of pride and thoughts from my past fueled my anger.

"Like I said, you were on your phone and moving too slow," Kelly replied.

"I don't care what I was doing," I spat. "I was here first, so you need to screw your little gas cap back on and get out of my way."

Kelly looked at me with the gas pump in her hand. "I don't know who you think you are talking to like that, but—"

Before she could even finish, I blacked out. In one swift movement, I grabbed Kelly by her neck and pushed her to the ground.

"Get *off* me you psycho!" she screamed.

I kept hitting her. Other pedestrians around us came running to her rescue.

"It was my goddamn turn!" I shouted hysterically just as someone scooped me up from behind, lifting me off of her.

All eyes were on us, but I didn't care. Kelly got up from the ground, quickly got in her car, and pulled away.

Huffing deeply, I yanked away from the big, hulk-looking man who was holding me and got into my car. I was *still* going to get my gas.

The next day, I saw line-cutter Kelly walking out of the student center. She stopped dead in her tracks when we locked eyes and hurried back into the building. I kind of felt bad. The look on her face was nothing but fear. That was the last thing I wanted to portray. I knew how it felt all too well.

Chapter 18

During winter break, I went home to see Sugar. I hadn't seen my friend in almost three months. We had a lot of hanging out to do. Our church was holding its annual conference at the Valley Forge hotel. It was always a huge event. The conference lasted for four days, and all the youth from different states would be there, showing off in their suits. Brian played the piano at his church and was set to play at the opening conference night. Sugar and I made plans to go watch him do his thing.

I pulled up at Sugar's house and honked my horn for her to come outside. She popped out five minutes later, smiling from ear to ear.

"Missy, hey!" She ran to get in the car.

"Hey!" I reached over to give her a hug. "It doesn't seem like I've been away for three months. You still look the same, and you have the same weave you had when I left." I laughed.

"I do not." She playfully hit my arm. "This is a different color."

"Where's Casey?" I asked, pulling off. "I miss my baby."

"She's with my godmother. They went to Ocean City for the week."

"Oh no, I won't even get to see her. I have to go back to school next Tuesday."

"Yeah, she won't be back until next Thursday."

"Aww, man."

"Girl, you look so much slimmer." Sugar looked at me. "You've got your hair all done up—and are those *heels*?" She tried looking down at my feet.

Blushing, I refused to look at her. "Maybe."

She burst out into laughter. "Look at you trying be cute for *Brian*."

"Yeah, yeah." I shook my head, embarrassed.

"So, how's school? Anything new other than the stuff you tell me every day?"

"No. I wish you were up there. I made a few friends and study partners, but I don't seem to click with anyone there like I do with you."

"You still beating people up over gas?" Sugar laughed. "What happened to that girl from the gas station?"

I laughed and shook my head. "She's around. She was friends with my roommate Jazmin, so that altercation sparked a lot of tension between her and me. Jazz doesn't really talk to me anymore—not that I care. I don't like her or her snotty group of friends. It just sucks that I have to live with her. We speak when we need to, and she's never really in the room any more. I just can't wait until next semester, so I can switch dorms. I'm in an all-girls dorm now, and it's always drama stirring up with all the girls."

"Really? Like in high school?" Sugar asked.

"Girl, it's worse than high school. They get into arguments and break into each other's rooms. The roommates get into fights with one another. In the mornings, the showers are always crowded, and the girls get mad and keep flushing the toilet to make the water cold. It's a mess. I can't wait to get out of there." I laughed. "But other than that, things are good."

We continued to catch up and laugh for the duration of our trip. When we arrived, service had already begun. We found two seats in the back and sat down. I spotted Brian over by the piano playing. He was such a cutie. At twenty-two, he had a lot going for him. The upcoming semester would be his last, and he'd already told me his plan to pursue a master's degree.

Brian had a milk chocolate skin tone with a skinny frame. He stood about six feet tall and had the smile of an angel.

"That man *sure* can play the keyboard," Sugar whispered to me.

Nodding my head, I chuckled. "Yeah, he *is* good."

"And I don't remember him being that attractive." She laughed. "I wonder if he has a brother."

Hearing Sugar talk that way was weird. She was just as shy as I was when it came to guys. We had both still been virgins and up until a few months ago, neither of us had ever had boyfriends. We'd had crushes and eye candy, but never went out on any dates and had never been kissed. Now, I was dating, and she was still single.

My phone vibrated in my bag so I reached down and looked at it. It was a text from Brian.

Hey pretty lady. Meet me in the hall by the bathrooms. I want to see you.

Sugar and I read the text and smirked.

"I'll be back." I got up from my seat. Brian had gotten up from the piano as well. I walked out into the hallway by the bathrooms and waited for him. For some reason, I was so nervous. After four months, Brian still gave me butterflies whenever he was around me. He walked up to me smiling with his pearly white teeth and fitted gray suit.

"Hey you." He reached out and grabbed me. When he pulled me into his arms and stole a quick kiss, my heart fluttered.

"Hey Brian." I tried my best not to blush.

"You look amazing." He stared me down. "I'm digging those heels."

"Thanks."

We stood out in the hall for about fifteen minutes talking. As we laughed and chatted away, I noticed a short, heavyset woman who looked to be in her early thirties walking back and forth past us to get into the ladies room. She had to have come back and forth in our direction about three times, putting an extra emphasis on the words *excuse me* each time she walked by. After the fourth time she walked past, I figured maybe Brian and I were standing too close. It was probably her way of telling us to break it up outside of the church.

"Maybe we should get back inside. We can finish talking after church," I told him.

"Cool. You and Sugar wanna come out to eat with me and the band?"

"Yeah, sure. I'll see if she's up for it."

After a quick hug, we both walked back into service. When I got to my seat, I looked for the woman to see if I knew anyone she was sitting near. I couldn't seem to find her, but as I was whispering to Sugar about her, she was actually being introduced as the soloist for the service and was walking up on the stage to sing.

"That's her," I said to Sugar.

"I've never seen her before. Maybe she has a UTI or something," Sugar said and we both laughed.

We had no idea who she was, but she sure could sing. When the woman was finished, she went back to her seat, and I could see her eyeing me from time to time. At one point, she glanced over at Brian too.

"Why does she keep looking at you like that?" Sugar asked.

"I don't know—it's so weird. Maybe she's one of those strict church ladies who's against PDA," I said.

"Either way, she's pretty creepy."

"I know," I replied with a laugh.

Eventually, we let it go and thought maybe it was just a coincidence, and before the night was over, we had forgotten about the whole thing.

Chapter 19

A couple weeks later, I was back at school and on my computer. I was logged into Facebook and decided to leave a heart on Brian's page. When I went on his page to leave a comment, I noticed that same woman from the convention listed on his friends list. Her name was Mercedes, and she was actually the youth leader at his church.

"Oh," I said out loud. "This whole time she was the *youth leader*? That makes sense."

After that, I was actually a bit embarrassed. I was sure she was keeping a watchful eye on her youth that night, and there I was all up in Brian's face, hugged up by the bathroom. I hope she didn't think I was some kind of whore chasing after him. I decided to send her a message. I told her she had a beautiful voice and said I'd really enjoyed her performance. She replied back almost instantly.

Hello!!! Thank you so much! I've been singing since I was two years old. You wouldn't believe that I failed music class three years in a row. LOL. God is good!

I responded back, *Are you serious? That's crazy! Well I'm glad you finally passed, LOL. Your voice is amazing.*

She replied, *Again, thank you! I remember seeing you and your friend at the convocation. Who's your pastor?*

Pastor Phil, I replied. *We were planning to stay the whole four days, but we didn't have the money, so I just came for the one night to hear my boyfriend, Brian, play. I saw that you're the youth leader at his church.*

Oh! Brian. Yes, he's such a sweet guy and a good catch. I know him very well. Musicians are always a hot commodity within our district, so I'll be sure to keep my eye on him. You seem like such a sweet girl. I can sense even through messenger that you've got the spirit of God all over your life.

That was a shocking surprise. I'd never had someone tell me they felt God on me. That made me smile. She told me to keep in touch, and I said I would. I signed off of Facebook and prepared myself for my 1:30 PM class. Mercedes was a nice lady. I pulled out my phone to text Sugar and tell her about it. When I looked at my screen, I had a message from Brian saying good afternoon and asking me how my day was going. Brian wasn't back in school; he was doing an externship at Delaware State University that was required for graduation. I grabbed my schoolbag and walked out of my room, en route to my class and texting along the way.

*****

My conversation with Mercedes continued back and forth for a few days via Facebook messenger. She was very smart, very intelligent, and knew a lot about God. I thought maybe she'd be a good spiritual mentor. I started to ask her questions about church and different ways to get closer to God. She asked me for my number because she said she'd rather talk to me over the phone about that type of stuff.

I gave her my number and she called me later on that night and answered all my questions. Mercedes asked me about college life, and how long I had been a member of my church. She was interested in my spiritual walk and talked to me like a big sister.

"You've really grown on me, Missy. You remind me of a sponge that's ready to absorb anything. I love that about you. Most young people are the exact opposite. You can't tell them anything and they don't want to learn."

"I'm cut from a different cloth, I guess," I responded. "Anything about God, I'm always willing to learn about."

"I see that. I'm going to call you every week to check up on you. College is a great place for young people but can also be a death trap. Lots of open doors and different things to experience, some good, some not so good. I'm going to keep my eye on you." She laughed.

"No problem," I said. "I'd love that."

She did just that. She called me every week to check on me and ask me how I was doing. She'd talk to me about her life and all the wonderful things she had done. She sang with a group and they had recorded a CD. They also lived together for some time in a big house, but once they split up, she kept the big house for herself. I liked her a lot. I'd never had a mentor or anyone to look up to who could steer me in the right direction.

One night as we were talking, the other line beeped on my phone and I looked and saw that it was Sugar.

"Okay, well, my friend is on the other line, so I'll talk to you later," I said.

"Okay sure, good night."

"Good night," I said before clicking over to Sugar. "Hey girl."

"Negro, I text you like an hour ago and you never replied back," Sugar snapped.

"Sorry, I didn't see it—I was on the phone with Mercedes."

"Oh God, that creep woman again?" She laughed.

"She's not a creep." I laughed back. "She's actually really smart."

"She's a creep with a beautiful voice," Sugar responded.

"Beautiful voice is right. You know she failed music class three years in a row? She was saying how God just kept blessing her and anointing her to sing even when she failed to practice. You've got to hear the way she talks about God. I hope I'm that spiritually knowledgeable when I get that old."

"That *old*? How old is she?"

"Her Facebook says she's thirty-one." I shrugged. "So anyway, are you coming up this weekend?"

"I want too," Sugar said. "If I can get some money from my grandmom."

"Well, if I can get some money from my grandmom for gas, I'll come get you, or I'll just come to Philly," I replied.

"Okay cool."

My phone beeped in my ear. It was a text from Brian telling me he was thinking about me.

"Brian just texted me." I blushed.

"Oh Lord, I can feel you smiling from ear to ear. *Loser*," Sugar joked.

"Oh, I found out his younger brother *is* single." I laughed.

"He's probably ugly." She laughed. "No thanks."

"I'm getting ready to look on Facebook to see if Brian has pictures up of him, so I can see what he looks like."

As I got on my computer to log on to Facebook again, my other line beeped, and it was Mercedes... *again.*

"Hang on a sec," I told Sugar before clicking over. "Hello?"

"Hey," Mercedes said. "You got a minute? I wanted your opinion really quick on this new song I'm writing."

"Well I was talking to Sugar about Brian's younger brother, but I can call her back."

Mercedes laughed. "Who, Jovan?"

"Yeah..."

"Oh," she teased, "Sugar's interested in him?"

Laughing, I replied, "Maybe."

"He's a little cutie," Mercedes replied. "She'd like him."

"Well, if he is anything like his brother, I know she would."

"You really like Brian, don't you?"

"Do I?" I found myself smiling. "Yes!"

There was a dead silence on the other end of the phone for about ten seconds.

"Missy," she said, hesitantly, "I have to tell you something."

I stopped typing on my computer. The obvious change in her tone alerted me. She sounded worried, and it didn't sit too well with me.

"I don't like the way you said that," I said. "Please don't tell me he has another girlfriend."

Mercedes took a deep breath. "Brian and I have been sleeping together off and on for the past two years. He is *not* a good guy. Don't let the church-act fool you. Brian has a couple of other girls I found out about. He is a lying, cheating, manipulative dog."

Pulling the phone away from my ear, I looked at it with confusion. *Did I just hear her correctly?*

"Come again," I said into the phone.

"I know I should have said something to you in the beginning, but I had no idea you would turn out to be such a sweet, innocent girl. When you reached out to me that day on Facebook, I was shocked. I don't pry in Brian's business. What he and I have is just that. I take it for what it is. I never expected to get close to you or take you under my wing. You grew on me very fast, and it's been eating me alive."

I sat at my desk in complete and utter silence as my mind tried to piece together what had just happened. Mercedes didn't seem like Brian's type at all. She was so much older than him, she had a very old motherly spirit, and he was the *last* person I would consider to be a lying, cheating, manipulative dog. All of a sudden, everything began to make sense. It wasn't a coincidence that she kept walking past us that night at the convention center.

Ain't this a bitch…

Chapter 20

"*Sleeping with him*? Are you *serious*?" Sugar's high-pitched tone screamed into the phone

"I feel so stupid." I shook my head.

My other line beeped, and I saw Mercedes's name flashing. I'd hung up on her after she told me the situation, and she'd called me back about five times. I refused to answer. I hit the ignore button and continued talking to Sugar.

"*But how*?" Sugar asked. "Well I know *how*, but she doesn't even seem like his type. These accusations don't sound like Brian at all."

"Same thing *I* said. She told me they were in a relationship for years and they broke up because he could never stay faithful. I'm guessing they were broken up while we were dating, which explains her scoping me out at the convention.

"This is crazy. They have you tangled up in some kind of love triangle." Sugar laughed.

"She seemed so genuine, though." I still couldn't wrap my mind around it.

"I *told* you she was a creep," Sugar blurted out. "I knew something was off about her. I like the fact that she's intelligent and knows about God, but you have to be careful. The devil knows about God too. He *was* an angel once."

"My defenses were really down with this one. She has such an old soul, like a church mother. She even dresses like she's on the mother's board...this is just crazy," I replied in disgust.

"Does Brian know you guys have been talking?"

"I don't think so. He's been texting and calling me every day. When we were at the convention center and she kept walking past us, he didn't even acknowledge her."

"Are you going to say something to him?" Sugar asked.

"No. I just want them both to leave me alone. This is too much for me."

"Yeah, I feel you."

"And here she is calling me back again." I huffed as Mercedes's name popped up on my call waiting again. "I'm not answering."

"Maybe you should see what she has to say for herself."

My other line continued to beep.

"Answer her," Sugar told me. "Like, at least get some closure."

"I don't think I really want to dig any deeper, but all right." I sighed. "I'll call you back."

I answered the other call and as soon as we got connected, Mercedes quickly began talking in an attempt to defend herself.

"Missy, I'm so sorry," she pleaded. "I am so, so sorry. Please don't hang up on me, just let me explain."

"I'm listening..."

"I didn't think it was my business to put him out there. I've felt horrible about keeping Brian and me a secret. I've been trying to find a way to tell you since last week. We aren't together anymore and have been broken up for a couple months because he's always with another woman. I've even slowed down on our sexual relationship. I couldn't care less about him now. I would still like to keep in contact with you. You've really grown on me, I mean that, and I would hate for you to turn into an enemy over a guy."

I did like Mercedes a lot and was beginning to trust her, but after this stunt she'd pulled, I wasn't sure if I should.

"I forgive you, but I don't trust you anymore," I said. "I've never had a mentor before, and I genuinely thought God had placed you in my life to teach me something positive. This is all a big mess now. I really liked Brian. This is weird, and very uncomfortable. I don't know what to say to either of you. Does he know we've been talking?"

"Not that I know of. The last time I spoke to him was at the convention center."

"Yeah...when you kept walking in between us to get to the bathroom?" I rolled my eyes.

"Yes, because he had just been over at my house earlier that day talking about how he missed us, and then he pops up at the convention with you. I gave that boy two years of my life...my love, my intimacy, and each time I have been made to look like a fool. We broke up every month it seemed like, and he always comes back apologizing, wanting to fix things. I don't know why I fall for it every time. I could be doing so much with my life, but year after year I have waited for him to get himself together and he refuses. I can't do it anymore, and now he has dragged a young, beautiful, innocent girl like you into this mess." She began to cry.

As I listened to Mercedes on the other end of the phone, I felt bad for her. We seemed to have known two different people. Listening to her cry like that pulled on my heartstrings. *Guys are such jerks.* She continued rambling on and on about different situations in which Brian completely disrespected and played her for a dummy. Those stories turned me completely off. At first, I didn't want anything else to do with *her*, but now I didn't want anything to do with *him*. I wanted to dump him and never see him again. It had been fun while it lasted, but I wasn't ready for love, especially not the kind she was describing.

"Listen," she said, "I'm not sure if you believe me but—"

"I forgive you," I cut her off. "Let's just put this whole thing behind us. You're right, we have grown on each other these past couple weeks. I can't continue a relationship with the both of you, but what it all boils down to is that cheating guys are everywhere. Genuine people with good hearts and good intentions are very hard to come by. I believe you, and I want you to continue mentoring me. Forget him."

"That makes me feel so much better." Mercedes sounded relieved. "But how can we sweep this under the rug? I don't want Brian to know I was the one who ratted him out. It would start a bunch of trouble and I would be caught in the middle of it. Are you sure you want to dump him? I don't want to be the center of any drama."

"Don't worry, there won't be any."

Later on that night when Brian called me, I gave him the news. I told him our relationship wasn't working, and said I realized he wasn't the nice guy I thought he was. He got furious and wanted to know who'd gotten into my head and fed me a bunch of lies about him, but I didn't respond to his questions. I said what I needed to say, and I hung up the phone. Brian called me back one hundred and fifty-two times and sent me seventy-eight text messages. I never responded.

Chapter 21

A couple weeks went by, and I was really beginning to like Mercedes. I loved that she knew so much and could teach me about life in general. One night, she pulled my card and asked me about my parents. After she'd told me about her wonderful life, I was embarrassed to tell her that I was practically homeless. I almost lied and made up some crazy story, but I felt like I owed it to her to be honest.

I told her about my entire life, where I came from, and how I got to college. There was a complete silence on the other end of the phone when I finished talking and I thought she'd hung up on me. After a minute she finally spoke. She told me my personality didn't match my history. She told me I was a good girl and she felt so bad that I had gone through all that. She told me she wanted to be a mother to me, and that if I needed a place to stay, she had a big house she lived in alone and I was welcome to come live with her, rent-free. She told me I didn't need to pay for anything, said she would take care of everything I needed while I was in college.

This was a first. Most of the homes I'd lived in growing up were full of people who only took me in because they were doing a favor for someone else, or they knew they'd be getting a check from the state. I'd never had anyone actually welcome me into their home, offer to be a mother to me and take care of me. I was so overwhelmed and excited because a mother and a home was what I'd always wanted. Before I gave her a definite answer, I called up Sugar and told her what had happened. Sugar was in the middle of eating dinner and almost spit her food across the table.

"Don't you *dare* go live with her. I don't like her. There's something fishy about that woman, and if I were you, I wouldn't stick around to figure it out. First, she got you to dump Brian and not give him an answer as to why. Now she wants to play mommy and invite you into her home and take care of you? No. *Don't do it.* It's a trap."

"Sugar, you don't know how it feels to have love, attention, and stability dangling in your face. I've always had to watch others enjoying that stuff from a distance and I've always wanted to know what it felt like." Tears welled up in my eyes.

"I understand but be careful. The enemy is waiting for an opportunity to trick you. His gateway is usually the thing that controls your emotions, decisions, and even your integrity. Don't get caught up in your fleshly desires. Don't go back and allow people to hustle you for your future in return for fake love, appraisal, and shelter. It's *not* worth it. Keep moving forward. Forget what you lost. In time, God will replace it all. Do *not* sell your soul to the devil," Sugar warned.

"I hear you," I said softly.

"Listen, it's your decision and I'm always going to be your best friend, regardless. Just be careful."

"Thanks Sugar. I'll call you up tomorrow, it's been a long day. I'm gonna go to bed."

"Cool. Talk to you tomorrow." We both said our goodnights and ended the call.

Sugar was right. Everything she said was true. I was so confused and torn. This woman seemed so nice, minus the whole Brian situation. Was it really worth giving her a chance?

I tossed and turned all night, and when I woke up the next morning, I decided I would try it. I wasn't going to move in right away—I wanted to see her and feel her out first. She'd already manipulated me once, and I didn't want to get played for a fool twice. That weekend, she invited me to come stay the night, and I agreed, but only if I could bring Sugar with me. She said it was okay and I begged Sugar to come, but she wasn't interested. Sugar was never a fan of being around anyone she didn't feel comfortable with. I was sad I had to go alone, but I bit the bullet and went anyway.

Mercedes was very welcoming. She treated me exactly how she spoke to me over the phone: motherly, respectful, and sweet. Her home was absolutely beautiful. I thought she was rich. She had a four-bedroom, two-bathroom single family home with a huge front and back yard, a big basement, and a huge den. I couldn't believe she lived there all by herself. I'd have been terrified of having that much house living alone. All the noises would scare me.

I stayed the whole weekend and Mercedes took me out, cooked all my favorite foods, and spent time telling me about God. It almost felt too good to be true.

That Sunday I ended up going to church with her. As soon as we walked in the door together, Brian—

as dark skinned as he was—turned a flushed red tint in the face. He waited until I was sitting alone and came over to ask if we could talk.

"How do you know Mercedes?" he asked sharply.

"Hello to you too." I rolled my eyes.

"Well, for the past three weeks all my *hellos* and *how are you's* have been ignored, so I figured we were past that. But really, how do you know Mercedes? I've never seen you two together before, and it's ironic how things were good between us, and now all of a sudden you're with *her* and you hate *me*."

"I don't hate you. I just don't think we fit together, that's all. I really don't want to talk about it. You're a great guy, just not for me, and it has nothing to do with Mercedes," I said, flat-out lying in church.

He looked at me and shook his head. After a few minutes of sitting there feeling stupid, Brian got up and moved to another seat. Later on that night, Mercedes and I went out to dinner and I received a long text message from Brian.

Mystery, I really liked you. From day one, you were different than most girls. We were having such a good time, and I've been trying to wrap my mind around who would tell you such lies about me in an attempt to ruin my character. When I saw you walk into church earlier with Mercedes, suddenly it all came together. I slept with her a couple times, but that was it. I was never interested in being in a relationship, showing her off in public, or giving her the love she wants so badly. I just wanted sex and as long as she kept giving it to me, I kept taking it. She started stalking me and badgering me about being in a relationship. I kept giving her the runaround because I didn't want to be with her, but I also didn't want to hurt her feelings. She's not my type at all. When she finally began to see me being open with my relationships and expressing them publicly, she got pissed off. She purposely got close to you to find out who you were, and then manipulated you into dumping me. She still thinks she has a chance with me. You don't have to respond. I'll leave you alone from here on out, but for the record, I was never the dog she probably made me out to be.

I read Brian's text message in silence as I sat at the table with Mercedes. I honestly didn't know who to believe.

"Who's that texting you?" Mercedes asked.

"Oh, just Sugar telling me something about her dad." I stuffed my phone in my bag. I wanted to believe Brian, but in that moment, I felt like I needed a mom more than a boyfriend. I deleted his number, ignored his text message, and went on with my life. The next couple of weekends I found myself less focused on school and spent more time driving the three hours to and from Philly to hang out with Mercedes. She and I had such a good time. I begged Sugar every weekend to come over, and one weekend, she and Casey finally came. We all had so much fun. We talked, we laughed, and we enjoyed the company of a mother figure that we all wanted. After that weekend, Sugar's opinion of Mercedes changed. She liked Mercedes as well.

Shoot, if someone was willing to play the role of my mother and treat me the way I deserved to be treated, I figured I should definitely move in with her—and that's exactly what I did.

Words couldn't describe how good it felt to be taken care of with no strings attached. I loved it there so much that I didn't want to go back to school. I began to find myself disinterested in my schoolwork and campus life. Shippensburg was now too far away from home. The life of my car was ruined from the hundreds of miles I drove each week. I missed all my Friday and Monday classes, so I could get home earlier and stay longer.

Between being homesick and wanting to spend more time with Sugar and Mercedes, I ended up dropping out of college at the end of my junior year.

Chapter 22

"I can't believe you dropped out," Casey scolded as we sat in my living room waiting for Sugar to get dressed so we could go to the mall. "All that hard work, and you're going to just quit."

"I didn't *quit*," I corrected. "I'm transferring to Cheyney University. I already sent my paperwork in. I'm just waiting to hear back from them."

"Girl, you dropped out." Casey laughed. "Cheyney is *not* a real school."

"It is a great school with a great psychology program. Plus, I'll be closer to—"

"Don't beat my head with the bullshit." Casey laughed.

I gave her the side eye. That girl had really gotten loose with the lips over the years.

"It is a ghetto school," she continued. "You did three years of work from a good school, and now you're going to get your degree from a *ghetto* school—but you're right, at least you'll be closer to home." She laughed obnoxiously.

"I didn't like Ship anyway," I lied. "It's such a small town with nothing to do, and the malls are the worst. I'm glad to be transferring. Plus, I can get back involved with church."

"What did Mercedes say about you transferring?"

"She's all for it. As long as I get my degree, she doesn't care."

"Nope. Momma don't care. As long as you walk across somebody's stage, it's all right with me." Mercedes emerged down the stairs. "I'm getting ready to put a load of clothes in the washer, and then I'll be ready to go. Where's Sugar?"

"Upstairs, *still* getting dressed." Casey was clearly annoyed.

"Well, hopefully she'll be down within the next ten minutes." Mercedes headed to the basement.

"It must be nice to finally have a home. I really like Mercedes, and I love seeing you smile more often," Casey said.

"Yeah. It's nice. I'm glad I made the decision I did," I said. "So what's up with you? How are things at home?"

"A mess. My dad has been trying to step up. He wants me and Sugar to come live with him."

My eyebrows dipped in confusion. Sugar had never told me that, and we always told each other everything.

"Well, what happened?" I asked her.

"Sugar didn't want to go, but I went to his house." Casey shook her head. "I wasn't there but two hours before he started yelling at me."

"He hit you?" My eyes grew big.

"No." Casey jerked her head. "I said he yelled at me, I didn't say he was *crazy.*"

Relieved, I sighed.

"I don't know when that man is going to get it together," she said, "but hey, I'm not waiting around for it. After we got into an argument, he made me get out and go back with my grandma."

"What if you came to live with Mercedes and me?" I asked.

Casey looked up at me with those big beautiful bright eyes.

"Really?"

Living with Mercedes was like heaven on earth. It was only three months into the summer, but since I'd been home, she'd taken us all out to restaurants, she took us on vacations, road trips, to beaches, amusement parks—*everywhere*. Things were also looking up for me. She taught me how to deal with my pain in ways other than cutting my arms. My appetite was normal again, and we came up with an exercise schedule to help control my weight.

Although part of me didn't want to share my new home or my mentor, I loved Casey. I refused to allow my selfishness to keep her from experiencing the joys of having a great home.

"Yeah. You deserve to be happy. I know how it feels to want better and not be able to find it." I smiled.

Casey sat up in her chair and smiled. "Will Mercedes let me?"

"I'll ask her." I got up from the couch and proceeded to walk toward the basement. "In the meantime, go see what's taking Sugar so long."

"Okay."

I walked into the laundry room where Mercedes was unloading clothes from the dryer.

"Hey you," she said. "You ladies ready?"

"Yeah...well, Case and I are ready," I said.

Mercedes laughed.

"I have something I need to ask you."

"What is it?" She looked at me.

"Can Casey come stay with us until she graduates high school?"

Mercedes eyes got really big. "What? Why does she need to come stay with us?"

"Her dad wants to take her back. She doesn't want to go, but she feels her grandmother needs a break."

Mercedes paused. "I don't know. I don't really know her that well. She's a minor—she can't just move out and into some random woman's house."

"That's my best friend's little sister, and she's just as important to me as Sugar. I asked you because I know you can mentor her and protect her the way you do me. And let's be honest, you barely knew me when I moved in."

Mercedes looked at me, and she could tell I was serious. She knew I was speaking from my heart.

"All right, Missy, I'll think about it. How about we all discuss it at dinner?"

"That's fair," I responded.

Mercedes laid the rest of the clothes on the table and walked upstairs into the living room. I followed behind her. Sugar had finally come downstairs and was standing by the front door.

We all walked outside and into Mercedes's car. I didn't know how Sugar would react to this, but we were about to find out.

"So, there's been some discussion about Casey coming to live with me," Mercedes started.

Sugar looked up from her phone and looked at Casey then at me. "What?"

"Sugar, I don't want to live with Daddy, and you know Grandma needs time to herself. We are not her kids...she needs a break."

"I'm open to it, as long as it's okay with your grandmother," Mercedes added. "I'd like to meet her."

Sugar took a deep breath and rolled her eyes.

"What's wrong?" I asked.

"Nothing is wrong. Casey can do what she wants. Don't expect me to move here, though—I'm not leaving my grandmother by herself."

"That's fine, you don't have to," Casey said.

"That's because I know the importance of being there for your *family*," Sugar snapped back at her sister.

"No, it's because Grandma likes you better than me," Casey responded.

"Oh my God. Whatever Casey, just shut up. If you want to move here, move here. I don't care."

But she did care. Sugar loved her sister. She was a very humble girl that stayed away from drama and trouble. She didn't care what kind of mess she was in, Sugar always found a way to be happy in it. She didn't like the fact that her baby sister would be moving in with us. While Casey and Sugar were always over at my house anyway, it was the principle of Sugar feeling like her sister was leaving her to move in with other people that hurt the most. If the shoe were on the other foot, Sugar would have *never* done that.

"Just go," Sugar said. "Grandma and I will be just fine..."

Chapter 23

"This dress is so cute." Sugar held up a pink dress. "What do you think?"

"It's cute...for *your* tiny butt. They don't make anything in here for girls with hips." I laughed.

Sugar and I had been shopping all afternoon. A few months had passed since Casey moved in with me and Mercedes. Sugar vowed she'd never move in, and even though she didn't, she was with us all the time.

"You are not big," Sugar said, "and they have dresses in a large to fit you. I don't know if it would fit over that big butt of yours, but it would certainly fit your upper body."

We both laughed as she continued sifting through the rack of summer dresses. Our church was having a dinner to honor our pastor's wife, and neither one of us had anything cute to wear. Just as I began searching through a rack of shirts, my phone rang. It was Mercedes.

"Hey," I answered.

"Hey honey, listen, Casey wants to go out to dinner instead of going with you tonight. She said they can't cook over there at your church." Mercedes laughed. "I'm just going to drop you two off and Casey and I will go to Red Lobster. Are you guys finished at the mall?"

"Mercedes, you've known about this for a month now, and you said you would go." I was instantly annoyed. "Now, because Casey is against it, you're going to drop us off and take her somewhere else?"

"I'm not a member of your church. Technically, I don't have to go anywhere or do anything they ask me to do. I don't feel like getting dressed up and putting on heels anyway. *Also*, I shouldn't have to explain myself to *you*. I'm the parent, you're the child," she reminded me.

"Whatever." I rolled my eyes.

"Casey and I are getting dressed now, so can you hurry back with the car? Make it within the next twenty minutes."

"The dinner doesn't start until 8 o'clock. It's 5:30," I fussed.

"I know what time it is. Casey and I will probably catch a movie beforehand, so I'll be dropping you guys off at the church a little early. If no one's there, I'll take you both to Sugar's grandmother's."

Listening to Mercedes talk was beginning to make me so mad. Ever since Casey moved in, I noticed a slight shift in her focus. I mean, don't get me wrong, I loved Casey, but the way Mercedes catered to her really annoyed me. She didn't make Casey clean the house the way she assigned me chores. If Casey didn't want to eat a certain meal that Mercedes had prepared, she didn't have to. In fact, she would make a completely separate meal at Casey's request.

"Okay, bye." I hung up the phone and folded my arms.

"Mercedes isn't going to the dinner anymore?" Sugar asked.

"No, she's not going because your sister doesn't want to go. They're going to do their own thing, and now she wants her car back."

"Well, I can just get this dress here. You still haven't found anything, though," Sugar added.

"It's fine. I'll just wear something old in my closet," I responded. I really didn't care anymore.

I stormed out of the store headed for the nearby bench. It wasn't fine at all. I was so hurt. It wasn't the first time Mercedes blew us off to go spend time with Casey. I was really beginning to resent that little girl, but I dared not say it in front of Sugar. Just as I stepped out of the store, I bumped into the most handsome man I had ever seen.

"I'm sorry." I gasped as he stretched his hands out to stop our impending full-on collision.

"It's fi—" He looked up at me, and his bottom jaw slightly dropped. "It's fine." He stumbled to get the rest of his words out. His complexion was midnight brown and coffee ground smooth. His face was so strong and defined, his features looked as if they were molded from granite. He looked to be about six feet tall with muscles that rippled through his fitted t-shirt. His soft, sharp lips were so captivating, I almost wanted to kiss them to see how they felt. His piercing eyes were full of intensity, alluring and seductive. I'd never seen anything so beautiful. It was as if God had carefully structured him just to spoil my eyes.

"You look familiar." The man with the velvet voice studied me, trying to figure out where he'd seen me from. "Do you go to Cheyney University?"

"I do," I confirmed. "Well, not yet, but I was there a few weeks ago for orientation."

"You were." He smiled at me. "You were sitting with a lady a few rows in front of me."

"I was?" I asked. I tried to keep my words brief so he couldn't hear the shaking in my voice.

"I'm Jordan." He extended his hand. "I graduated last year, but I work full time with the track team. I have a dorm up there for the summer and next semester."

"I'm Mystery." I shook his hand.

"Really? That's your real name?" He looked amused.

"What's so funny?"

"Nothing. I've just never met anyone named Mystery before."

"Me either." I gave him the side eye.

"I like it. It's different."

"All my friends call me Missy," I said.

"Well I like Mystery better. Missy sounds too common. Just like your name, you stand out. I'd rather call you by your name."

Slightly blushing, I shook my head to keep from fainting.

Sugar walked out of the store and up to us. "You ready?" She noticed Jordan and did an immediate double take.

"I'm ready. It was nice meeting you, Jordan."

"You too." He moistened his lips and smiled at me one last time. "Hopefully I'll see you back at Cheyney."

We parted and went in different directions.

"Who is *that*?" Sugar's mouth fell open as soon as we got far enough away.

"Some guy from Cheyney. He said he saw me and Mercedes at orientation."

"He's *so* chocolate," she said.

"He sure is. Gives me a *toothache* just looking at him." Sugar and I shared a laugh.

Ten minutes later, we arrived back at my house. Casey and Mercedes were in the living room waiting for us to get back.

"Hey guys," Casey greeted.

"Hey," Sugar and I replied in unison.

"What did you get?" Mercedes asked.

"Well I got nothing since I was rushed." I cut an annoyed glance in Mercedes's direction. "Sugar got a dress."

"You and your spoiled ways." Mercedes rolled her eyes. "I'm tired of it. The world does not revolve around you. *Get over it*."

"It never did, and it never will," I shot back. "It's all about you and Casey now."

"Whatever. I don't have time for your unappreciative attitude," she said. "Grow up."

Ignoring her comment, Sugar and I went upstairs to get dressed for the dinner. She looked absolutely stunning in her pink dress that fell just past her knees. She topped it off with a pair of black heels and a black clutch. I put on a black dress that went just below my calves and black heels to match. I grabbed my black strapless purse, and Sugar and I headed down the stairs.

"Oh wow," Mercedes said. "Look at you, Sugar. You look *amazing*." Her eyes traveled Sugar's entire body. "You're ready to show off today, huh?"

"Something like that." Sugar blushed. "Missy looks beautiful, too." Sugar looked at me. "You and those hips. I'm *so* jealous."

"I'm not feeling all that black." Mercedes looked at me. "You look like you're going to a funeral, and that dress is a little too formfitting for a church event."

Sugar cut her eyes at me and then looked down at the floor. She knew I was pissed off and getting ready to flip out.

"If you didn't have anything nice to say about my dress, you could have kept it to yourself," I scolded.

Mercedes was headed for the front door, but she turned around to look at me instead.

"This is *my* house. I can say what I want in *my* house. *I* pay bills here, *not you*. If you don't like what I have to say, you can take your bags and *get out*, and if you do decide to leave, don't take anything I bought out of here with you, which leaves you with *nothing*."

"You're doing and saying this stuff on purpose." Tears surfaced in the cracks of my eyes. "It's like you can't be a mother to all three of us, you have to pick and choose who you like. You're being unfair and mean, and that's not right."

Sugar looked at me. I could tell she agreed, but she wasn't going to say anything.

"Missy, you're just used to having stuff your way. You need to watch how you talk to somebody who's taking care of you," Casey chimed in.

"Thank you, Casey." Mercedes put her hand on her hip.

"Wow. If this isn't the pot calling the kettle black," I muttered.

I was so upset and now felt uncomfortable in my dress that was apparently too formfitting. Mercedes had changed so much since Casey moved in with us, and I hated it. I turned around to walk back up the steps.

"Where you going?" Sugar asked.

"I'm not going. You go ahead, call me after the dinner." I walked into my bedroom and closed the door.

"Then don't go," Mercedes hollered. "Sugar if you don't want to go, there's always room for you to hang out with us."

"No. I'm going to the dinner," Sugar responded. "You can just drop me off at my grandmom's."

"Okay, no problem honey."

I heard their voices out the window until finally they disappeared into the car.

My anger rapidly flared. I sat on my bed and took off my shoes.

Now she puts me on the back burner, I thought. Privileges had been taken from me and given to Casey. I used to have a say-so in dinner requests, restaurant spots, and our agenda for the day.

I regretted having her come live with us. My relationship with my so-called mother was falling apart. Mercedes had not only turned on me, she was being manipulative as well. She realized we all longed for her affection and her attention, and she was using it to pit the three of us against each other.

She knew Sugar and I were like white on rice, and she often pulled little stunts like the one she just had about the dresses.

I felt like the ugly duckling and the evil stepdaughter living there. If I ever tried to stand up for myself, Mercedes would tell me I could leave and go back to being homeless. Threatening to kick me out became her way of control, because she knew I needed her. We all did. Mercedes became the ringleader in the circus. I should've never moved in there. I should have listened to Sugar.

Chapter 24

Over the next couple of months, I found myself regretting every decision I'd made to move in with Mercedes. The way she talked to me was ridiculous. I began classes at Cheyney University and my initial plan had been to stay on campus during the week and go home on the weekends. Needless to say, that didn't happen.

Mercedes purposely did things to try to tear Sugar, Casey, and me apart. During the weekends, she'd refuse to come pick me up and then would go out shopping or joyriding with Casey and Sugar. There were some weekends I found a ride home on my own, or I caught the bus. I really missed Sugar and would be so excited to hang out with her. When I'd get home, however, Mercedes would claim to have already made prior plans with Sugar and Casey that didn't include me, so I would be in the house alone.

Mercedes was so cold toward me, but she always had smiles and love for my friends. She'd shower them with motherly affection to my face then tell them how much of a troublemaker I was. Meanwhile, *she* was the force behind all the trouble.

Soon, I found myself enjoying being on campus more. Sugar and I were still close; nothing ever changed between us. She didn't like what Mercedes was doing, but she also didn't like confrontation. On the weekends she knew I was alone, Sugar would come up to Cheyney and stay with me.

Cheyney was a breeze in comparison to Shippensburg. I had a lot of fun, and I made a lot of friends. None of them were as close as Sugar and I were, but they made my time at school very pleasant.

One day as I was walking to the cafeteria while texting Sugar, I accidently bumped into Jordan. When I looked up and saw it was him, I smiled. We'd been cordial since the semester started, and he always found a way to run into me and spark up conversations.

"Mystery," he said flirtatiously, "how are you?"

"Hey." I smiled. "I'm good, and you?"

"Better now."

"Were you sick before?"

"No, just stressed a little bit. The track team isn't at all what I expected. They need a lot of training. Nothing I can't handle though."

"I'll bet." I giggled. "I've seen you run. You should totally try out for the Olympics. You move like lightning." My comment made him blush. He didn't realize I paid attention him, but I did—along with every other girl on campus.

"Where are you headed in such a rush?" He asked.

"I have to run up to the library to print out an assignment," I replied.

"I see...well, maybe we can hook up or something later on," he offered.

"Maybe we can." I grinned.

We exchanged numbers and parted ways.

I watched him as he walked off.

"That man is *so beautiful*," I mumbled under my breath. He made chocolate look *good*. My ringing phone cut through my thoughts. It was Sugar, and I picked up on the first ring.

"Guess who I just ran in to?" I asked excitedly.

"Who?" she asked.

"Jordan, the cute guy from the mall." I smiled. "And he finally gave me his number."

"Took you long enough. Don't you two go to the same school?" She laughed.

"Oh hush," I joked.

"Well, I was calling to inform you about Mercedes's birthday tomorrow."

"Oh," I replied dryly.

Sugar laughed. "Don't be like that. We have to do *something* for her. We should go to her house and surprise her tonight."

"Why tonight?"

"Because she may be expecting us to do something tomorrow. She's been working late this whole week since you've been at school, and Casey has been with me at my grandmom's because of her SAT prep classes, so Mercedes won't be expecting anything. We can get her a cake, hide out in her closet, and surprise her when she comes home."

I really wasn't interested in anything that had to do with Mercedes, but nonetheless, I figured it was fair for me to at least *pretend*.

"Okay cool. My classes are done for the day, so I can catch the bus into the city. What time does she get off?"

"She didn't say, and I don't want to ask because then it'll look suspect. We have keys. Let's just go there and wait."

"Sounds like a plan. I'll see what time the next bus leaves from here."

"Yay! Okay cool, see you then."

I felt like such a party pooper at times. Sugar and Casey loved Mercedes, but she had hurt me too bad for me to get that excited about her birthday. I had trusted her with all of my heart to look out for my best interest, which was hard for me to do considering my history with caregivers. Her house had been a house of peace, a place where I felt welcomed and taken care of, but now it was a house of drama and chaos, and I couldn't stand the sight of her.

I walked into the library to find Jordan and the rest of the track team sitting at the computers. As soon as he spotted me, a big grin spread across his face.

"Hello again," he greeted.

"This doesn't look like track practice."

"Coach canceled it because they're doing maintenance on the field, so we're having our practice in here today. Study hours."

"Sounds like fun," I replied.

"Plus, there was a certain someone I was hoping to run into."

I blushed.

"Do you need help printing out your paper? Jordan asked. "Maybe sit down and hang out for a while afterward?"

"Actually, I have to go home for a little bit. I need to grab a bus schedule."

"Bus schedules? Where do you live?"

"Well, I live in Jersey, but I'm meeting my best friend in Philly."

"I can take you if you'd like," Jordan said.

"Heck no, that's too much to ask. Besides, aren't you in the middle of study hours? I have to leave now if I'm gonna get home in time."

"It's my car, and I offered to drive you, so let me." Jordan stood up. "Plus, I am studying—*the female anatomy.*"

He grinned, studying me up and down before locking eyes with mine. I just laughed and shook my head.

"If it's not a problem, you can take me," I confirmed with a head nod.

"Great. Let's go."

I was pretty certain Jordan wasn't allowed to just get up and leave the library without his coach's permission, especially if he was supposed to be studying, but who was I to judge?

We walked out of the library to the student parking lot where his car was parked. When he pressed the button on his key and his car lights lit up, my mouth dropped open.

"You have a *Benz*?" I asked in shock.

"Yeah. It was a graduation gift from my mom. She got it for me last month.

"Wow. Most people get money or have graduation cookouts—your mom got you a Benz?"

I ogled the vehicle, admiring it.

"What can I say? My mother loves me. She's always down for spoiling her only son. When do you graduate?"

"This spring," I replied. Jordan opened the passenger door then shut it for me once I was inside. He walked across the front to the driver's side and got in.

"Here's the address." I showed him my phone. "You may want to put it in your GPS—I'm *horrible* with directions."

"Got it." Jordan turned on the car and proceeded to plug my address into his GPS.

"So are you *from* New Jersey?"

"No. I'm from Philly. I grew up in southwest, but I've lived in almost every part of the city."

"Wow." He looked shocked. "A Philly girl? I would've never guessed. You don't act anything like the girls from Philly."

"What's that supposed to mean?" I glanced at him, offended.

"Most of the Philly girls that go here are loud and ghetto. They have the multicolor weaves going on, and the skin-tight clothes. You seem really reserved. Your hair looks natural, and you're not wearing any makeup. I would've *never* guessed you were raised here." Jordan looked at me periodically while he drove.

"Yeah, I guess I'm a bit of a nerd. I don't drink. I don't smoke, I don't watch much TV, and I don't really date. I usually read books and hang out with my best friend."

"What you mean you don't really date?"

"I've only ever had one boyfriend," I admitted. "Some guy from my church district. I talked to him for about six months, but it didn't work out."

"He cheat on you or something?"

"Sources said one thing and he said another. My heart wasn't in it, he was just something to do. When the drama started, I backed out."

"That's amazing. You're a junior in college and you've only been in *one* relationship? You don't drink, you don't smoke, you don't party." Jordan laughed. "You're one in a million."

"Sorry if that turns you off." I shrugged. "But that's me. I'm simple."

"It doesn't turn me off. That's an amazing accomplishment. I knew something seemed different about you the first time I saw you. Everything about you screamed innocence. I wanted to get to know you the very first time I laid eyes on you. Seeing you at the mall was just confirmation."

"Confirmation of what?" I asked.

"That I had to have you, someday, at some point." Jordan smiled.

"Well, I don't know what you mean by *have* me, but I'm also a virgin, so if you're thinking you're going to—"

"Who said I wanted to sleep with you?"

"Oh..." I felt bad for jumping to conclusions. "That's usually what most guys are after."

"Well why can't I be different, just like you?" Jordan approached a red light and turned to look in my direction. "I'm so interested in you." His eyes bored into mine. "Every word that comes out of your mouth is like a breath of fresh air. You're probably one of the most beautiful girls I've ever met. I just want to know more."

I glanced at him for a quick second then turned away to look out the window. I was so embarrassed, but in a good way. I'd never had a guy talk to me like that, and I was extremely shy.

Jordan seemed so genuine. I was dying to know more about him almost as much as he wanted to know more about me, but I was too afraid to show it. After the situation with Brian, I didn't know if I was ready to trust another guy again. As I thought of what to say next, Jordan put his hand on my leg and moved up my thigh until he reached my hands, which were folded in my lap.

"Can I touch you?" he asked politely. "I don't bite."

"S-Sure," I replied, stuttering a bit. Jordan grabbed one of my hands and held it as he continued to drive. My heart began to beat so fast, I swore he could hear it.

We laughed and talked the rest of the way to my house. Jordan didn't feel comfortable dropping me off in Philly so he drove me all the way to New Jersey. I texted Sugar and let her know she didn't have to meet me, and that I would meet her at home.

During the drive, Jordan told me about his life and upbringing. He was from the suburbs, a fraternity boy, and loved working out and playing sports. I found out that his mother was actually a professor at our school. She taught social psychology, and I couldn't stand her. I would've never guessed Dr. Jackson had a charming, handsome son, considering she was so evil. I hated her class. I didn't think anyone who took it ever passed with more than a C. She was tough.

About fifteen minutes later, Jordan and I pulled up on my street. I told Jordan to drive around the back just in case Mercedes decided to pull up unannounced and spotted an unknown car in her driveway.

"Is this your mother you live with?" Jordan asked.

"No. She's more like a mentor to me. I met her a few years back.

"Where are your parents?"

"That's a story for another day." I shook my head.

We pulled up in the back of the house, and I took my keys out.

"No problem. Should I wait for you?" he asked.

"No, you don't have to. I'll probably be here a while and won't get back to school until late."

"Do you have a ride back?"

"Yes, the same way I was going to get here." I laughed. "The bus."

"Well, I don't want to intrude, but my day is pretty free since there's no practice. I don't mind sticking around to wait for you. It's silly to take a bus back to campus that late."

"Sure. You can stay if you want." I briefly thought about it. "I don't mind. You can meet my best friend Sugar and bodyguard the house since it's just us girls here." I chuckled.

Jordan playfully flexed his muscles. "I can do that."

Laughing, I replied, "You are so silly. Let's go."

We got out of the car and walked up to the back door. "You drove here like a bat out of *hell*, so I'm not sure anyone's even here yet."

I opened the door and walked in the basement with Jordan following behind me.

"This is a pretty neat spot." We walked up the steps into the living room. "It doesn't look this big from the outside, but this is nice!"

"Yeah, it's pretty co—"

A loud noise upstairs interrupted our conversation.

"What was that?" he asked.

"Probably Sugar and Casey. I figured we'd beat them here, but I guess not. Let's go scare them," I said softly as I began to creep up the stairs. "Follow behind me."

"They sure *will* be scared—they don't know me." Jordan chuckled.

"Even better. Let's go up to the hallway and hide behind the closet door. When I give the word, you jump out and freak them out."

The thought of seeing Sugar and Casey in fear made me snicker.

"So much for a first impression," Jordan whispered. "Are you sure?"

"It'll be fine. We do this stuff to each other all the time."

We reached the top of the stairs and tiptoed down the hallway. We took two steps before a few loud moans stopped us in our tracks.

"What the hell?" I whispered.

The moans got louder before a male voice began to grunt. The noises were coming from my bedroom.

"What in the hell is going on?" I was so confused. "Who's in my room?"

"Or *what* is in your room. That sounds like animals getting it on." Jordan snickered quietly.

"No, this is not funny." I walked slowly down the hall to my bedroom door.

Jordan followed me. When I approached my door, it was partially open. I looked inside to see Mercedes and Brian in my bed having wild, passionate sex. They were facing the opposite direction of the door, so they had no idea I was standing there. Jordan finally joined me, and his eyes widened in shock.

Brian sat upright on my bed, pulling Mercedes by the hair with one hand and grabbing her neck with the other while she grinded on him like a professional bull rider.

Quickly, I backed out of the doorway and hurried back down the steps. Jordan followed me, laughing quietly.

"Is that Sugar?" he asked.

"Let's go," I said angrily. I didn't even try to keep my voice lowered. I ran down the first flight of steps, and then the basement steps. Jordan hurried to catch up.

"What's wrong?" He looked confused. "Who were they?"

"It doesn't matter...we're leaving. Now!"

I walked to the back door and flung it open. Jordan unlocked his car and hurried to get inside. I slammed the back door with all my strength, got in the car, and slammed the door. Jordan started the car and sped off.

"Mystery, what's wrong? Who was that?"

"That was my mentor." I folded my arms across my chest.

"Well why are you upset?"

"The man she was sleeping with was my first boyfriend, Brian."

Jordan gasped. "No! Really?"

"Yes." Tears began to rush down my face.

"Wow." He laughed in shock. "What a *snake*. Do they know each other or something? Do you still like that guy? When you said mentor, I thought of an older woman. How did this happen?"

"No, I don't like Brian anymore." I shook my head. "I feel betrayed and lied to by someone who's supposed to be like a *mother* to me. Someone who once told me how horrible of a person Brian was, and said to stay away from him because he was no good. I dumped him because of her, and yet she's in my bed having sex with him."

Jordan remained quiet as I continued my rant. He drove in silence and put his hand on my leg to calm me down.

"I *hate* her. I never want to step foot in her house again." I sobbed. "She *knew* what she was doing all along. A word of advice for you, Jordan: when something seems too good to be true, it usually is."

Chapter 25

Two months later

I sat on my bed studying for my *Psychology of Personality* class, periodically glancing at the news on my television. Jordan sat next to me playing a game on his phone. Since the incident with Mercedes, I stopped going home period. I never answered any of her phone calls and always gave her excuses via text as to why I couldn't answer or wasn't coming home. As long as she knew I was alive, that was good enough for me. I told Sugar everything I saw that day. She couldn't believe it. She kept asking me if I was okay, and even though I said I was, she knew I wasn't. I let it go, however, because there was nothing Sugar or I could do about it. We weren't going to call Mercedes out on her dirt; we still needed her to take care of us.

I spent most of my time at school with Jordan. We hung out all day, every day, and I really liked him. He drove me to Philly a lot and went to church with me. He finally got the chance to meet Sugar, and she loved him. Since I stopped going over Mercedes's house on the weekends, Sugar stayed home more and kept herself busy with church. Casey stayed down in Jersey with Mercedes and they were basically inseparable.

Some days when I was finished with classes and Jordan was finished with the track team, we'd drive down to Philly and hang out with Sugar. Sugar and I introduced Jordan to my pastor and first lady. Over the next couple months, he became a really good friend to me and was just as fun to be around as Sugar. Everyone that came into contact with Jordan *loved* him. They were drawn to him. I saw it in the way they hung on to his words and reciprocated his smile so quickly. They want to be close to him just like I did. If he wanted to, he could've had more friends than hours in the day, but a small circle of friends was enough for him. Despite all the female attention that came his way, Jordan prized genuineness and thoughtful conversation above lipstick and high heels. He was handsome all right, but inside he was *beautiful.*

As I read the last page from my textbook, Jordan sat up and looked at me.

"So how do you feel about me?"

"Excuse me?" I peered up from my book.

"How do you feel about me?" he repeated. "Do you like me?"

"I...I do like you." I giggled at his innocence. "I think you're a really nice guy and I'm glad we're friends."

"I'm glad we're friends too, but I'd much rather you be my girlfriend." He caressed my cheek and took my textbook out of my hand. Immediately my heart began to thump. I liked Jordan just as much as he liked me, and I had been waiting for the day he actually asked me out. Some nights I'd go to bed imagining what the moment would be like when it actually came, and here it was.

"I d-do want to be y-your girlfriend," I said, stumbling over my words. "As long as you can look me in the eyes and swear to me that you don't have an older woman somewhere that you're sleeping with, who's gonna come hunt me down and beg to be my mentor when you piss her off."

"I swear I'm not." He laughed. "You're the only woman I'm after, and the only one I want."

Leaning in, Jordan gazed into my eyes with his dark piercing stare and kissed me. The moment his lips touched mine, I melted into his affection. *Is this really happening to me?* The hottest guy in school—the one all the girls wanted—wanted *me.* His lips tasted like heaven and when he wrapped an arm around my waist to get closer, I nearly passed out. Yes, it was *really* happening. *Jordan Jackson is mine.* Just as I moved my hand to secure it around his neck, my door flew open, causing both of us to jump.

"*Really* Jordan?" hissed an angry girl standing outside my door with her arms folded. "That's what you do when I graduate—you screw your groupies?"

Jordan's eyes nearly popped out of their sockets.

"Alana, what are you doing here?" He jumped down from my bed.

"I came here to surprise you on my day off," she folded her arms. "I knocked on your door and you weren't there. I was told you've been spending a lot of time with some *groupie*, and that her dorm room was probably where I could find you. So much for being a faithful boyfriend."

"Boyfriend?" I jerked my head back. "You've gotta be kidding me."

"No sweetheart, nobody is kidding." Alana shook her head with a smirk. "He's been mine for the last four years, so I don't know what you—"

"Mystery, wait. Let me explain something," Jordan interjected.

"No need. Your girlfriend here is doing all the explaining I need to hear." I got down off my bed.

"That's not the—"

"I can't *believe* you'd disrespect our relationship with a groupie," Alana screamed. "Four years means *nothing* to you?"

"Get out!" I screamed. "Both of you." I pushed Jordan toward the door and glared at Alana. "Before I put you out."

"*Put me out?*" She began to approach me. "I'd like to see that happen."

Jordan quickly moved in between us.

"Alana, you and I need to talk," he told her.

I walked behind them and grabbed my door handle. "But *not* in here."

Jordan looked back at me. I could see the embarrassment, guilt, and shame lingering in his eyes.

"Stay away from me," I said, staring into his eyes as he watched mine grow cold. I slammed the door so hard, it almost fell off the hinges. Tears immediately flooded my eyes and fell down my face. It was the second time in a row I'd been played by a guy, and this time was one I didn't see coming. Pressing my body up against the door, I slid down and began to cry. I was embarrassed and heartbroken. I couldn't *believe* him.

Was I some kind of joke? Why did this keep happening to me? Was there *anybody* other than Sugar who found me to be worth their time and effort?

As I shook my head and began to process what had just happened, I glanced up at the breaking news that popped up on the screen.

A deadly shooting broke out around 5 PM this evening on the 7200 block of Divinity Street.

That was Sugar's street. I wiped my face and stood up quickly to grab my cellphone.

"Oh my God." Frantically, I dialed her number while the news reporter continued with the developing story.

Witnesses say two men arguing over a basketball game quickly escalated into a shootout. Bullets rang out through the tiny block of Divinity Street injuring two, and possibly fatally injuring one. Police say sixteen-year-old Michael Stewart and nineteen-year-old Marcell Simpson were shot in the foot and arm and have been rushed to University Hospital where they are listed in stable condition.

"Oh my *God.*"

Marcell and Michael lived four doors down from Sugar. They were our friends who we hung out with often. I continued to watch in disbelief as I listened to the news reporter in one ear, the sound of Sugar's phone ringing in the other one.

Police also say twenty-one-year-old Sugar Johnson was shot in the head and also rushed to University Hospital where she is listed in critical condition.

The phone fell out of my hand and my heart nearly stopped beating. "SUGAR!"

Chapter 26

My nerves were through the roof as I rushed off the elevator at the University of Pennsylvania hospital. Mercedes was the first person I recognized in the waiting area. She was pacing back and forth, praying.

"Why didn't you call me and tell me what was going on?" I snapped at her. "This happened *hours* ago, and I just found out on the news!" My voice got the attention of everybody in the waiting room.

"Don't yell at me." Her snotty tone was elevated. "I was going to call you when I found out what was going on. I had to *get here* first."

"I h*ate* you," I hissed. "I swear...I hate you with a *passion*. You're going to bust hell wide open you evil, conniving, manipulative bi—"

Sugar's grandmother grabbed me by the arm. I hadn't even seen her sitting there.

Tears gushed out of my eyes.

"Calm down, it's all right. Walk with me." She ushered me down the hallway.

"I hate her so much," I cried. "She knew what she was doing. She was supposed to call me. I was supposed to know about this when it happened, not see it on the news."

"Missy, calm down *please*. Your temper won't make the situation any better," Sugar's grandmother said softly.

"Where's my friend?"

"She's in a coma. We've been here about five hours now. I thought someone called you and told you. I'm sorry."

"Coma?" My voice shook as my heart fell out of my chest and hit the floor.

"I'll walk you in to see her, but you *have* to calm down. She was outside on the steps and got hit with a stray bullet. She's in a coma, but she can still hear you, they say." Sugar's grandmother shook her head somberly. "All we can do at this very moment is give it to God and pray for a miracle. Please go in this room and encourage your best friend to come out of this. *Please…*"

My mind went in and out trying to grasp what was taking place. Sugar and I had *just* been together. The day before, we sat on her grandmother's steps reminiscing about a movie we saw. Now, she was in a coma. I walked toward her room in denial. *Maybe they were talking about another Sugar. It can't be my best friend. This can't be real. This is* not *real.*

Her grandmother walked me into her room, and there she was in a hospital bed, strapped to life support. Her brain was so swollen that it enlarged her head to the point where she didn't even look like herself. She was hooked up to all kinds of machines and wires. She looked like a vegetable. I choked out a cry and covered my mouth. I didn't want to see her like that, but I couldn't look away. All my life I'd never seen someone in a hospital before. The first time I did, it was my best friend

Her grandmother walked out of the room crying as tears continued rolling down my own face. *How the hell did this happen? Is she going to be okay?* I kept asking myself those questions.

After I stood there lifeless for about fifteen minutes, I finally walked up to the bed and reached for her hand.

"Sugar, what the hell did they do to you? Can you hear me? Are you in any pain? Are you asleep?"

No response. Every time I asked her a question and she didn't respond, it broke my heart. She was the only friend I had, and she was hurt, and there was nothing I could do to help her.

As I held Sugar's hand, a frenzy broke out in the hall. I let go of her hand and walked out to see what was going on. One of her cousins ran up to me, shaking frantically.

"Missy, they just said Sugar was brain dead and that they don't think she's going to survive."

I looked at everyone in the waiting room and hallway who were falling out and fainting at the doctor's news. It was all so overwhelming, and part of me thought I'd faint right along with them, but it was because of Sugar that I'd learned to trust in the power of God. My tears and worries came from me not being able to help her and not knowing if she was in any pain, but I certainly *knew* she wasn't going to die. That was just ridiculous. I served a God who'd kept me alive when I was nearly beaten to death by my mother. When I'd moved from home to home, he'd kept me protected. When I'd cut myself, he'd made sure I never cut an artery and bled to death.

With the kind of life I'd lived, I should've been in a mental institution or six feet under, but he kept me. I knew the same God that had saved *my* life was going to save *hers*.

I walked back into Sugar's room, closing the door behind me. I walked up to her and took her hand again.

"People are about to come in here screaming and hollering around your bedside. *Don't listen to them*," I said.

I watched the heart monitor that Sugar was hooked up to begin to elevate. I knew she could hear me.

"Sugar, don't freak out. I'm not going anywhere, I'm gonna stay right here. The doctors just told everybody that you weren't going to make it, but I don't believe them, and neither should you. We know who the *real* doctor is, so just hang on. Don't let these people's screams get to you."

Just as I reached in to hug her, her door swung open. Her mother, grandmother, and a host of aunts and uncles came bursting through.

The woman looked just like Sugar, a spitting image. I'd never met her before, but I knew she was Sugar's mother.

Casey and Mercedes came in as well. I pushed past them and walked out. I didn't want to be in there to listen to that. I walked down the hallway into a vacant waiting room. Sitting down, I put my hands on my head and I began to pray.

"Lord, my life has always been a pattern of ups, downs, and controversy. I remember praying to you in tears because I didn't understand why I had to endure so much pain. Sugar told me everything happens for a reason and said I should trust you. I listened to her because the way she spoke so highly of you led me to believe I really could trust you. She made me believe you could help me, and you did. You turned my life around, put me in a position to better myself, and you gave me a friend who made my life so much more pleasant. Through her, you showed me what real love and acceptance is, and since we've been together, we've been inseparable. My life is still chaotic, and sometimes I don't understand why things happen to me the way that they do, but I trust that everything that's happening right now is part of your plan. Please keep Sugar pain-free through whatever process you're trying to birth out of this. It breaks my heart to see my best friend like that, but I'm going to be strong, because no one else is at this point. I have faith in your ability, and I'm asking that you move quickly because I don't know how long I can watch her suffer like this. In Jesus' name, amen."

I sat in that waiting room for hours just thinking, trying to piece together everything that had taken place. I almost forgot about the situation with Jordan until I looked up and saw him standing in front of me.

"Are you okay? I rushed here as soon as I heard what happened." He sat down next to me.

"Yeah," I responded coldly, staring straight ahead. I didn't want to look at his dishonest ass.

"Can we talk?" he asked. "I know this isn't a good time and you probably don't even care, but I'm sorry for all of this. I *did* have a girlfriend. Alana and I have been dating since my freshman year of college. She graduated, and—"

"Jordan, I don't care." I stood up. "I don't care about you, your obnoxious girlfriend, or your sob story as to why you lied to me for almost three months. Sugar likes you—*for now*—so I won't be ignorant and make you leave. Her room is up the hall, so go see *her* and get away from *me.*"

Jordan stared at me. His eyes immediately filled with hurt, but I didn't care. He turned and walked away.

Four days later, I sat in the chair next to Sugar's bedside. I'd been sitting in the same spot off and on since the first day I got there. She was still in the coma, and I refused to leave her side. I didn't eat, I didn't sleep, and I barely went to the bathroom. I sat by her bed all day, and when the doctors came in to shut the lights off for the night, I asked for a blanket, so I could stay in the room with her. I didn't want her to wake up out of her coma and be by herself or not see anyone she knew. I talked to her, I prayed for her, I laughed and joked with her like we normally did, and I held her hand, so she could feel that I was there.

Everyone else was given courtesy hotel rooms that were attached to the other side of the hospital, but I wasn't staying in any of them. I wasn't moving until Sugar got up. My phone rang, and I looked and saw that it was my pastor's wife. I stood and walked out of the room to answer it.

"Hello?"

"Hey Missy, how are things up there?"

"Things are things," I said sadly. "Just waiting for her to wake up. She's been breathing on her own and slowly getting better, but they still have her hooked up to all these machines."

"I couldn't make it up there, but the pastor is there. He told me you've been sitting in the room this whole time with her," she said.

"Yeah, I don't want to leave her. If it were me, she wouldn't leave me here either."

"I know. You girls are two peas in a pod." She paused for a minute. "Everything is going to be okay. It's in God's hands now. Just keep praying and encouraging her. She'll wake up any minute."

"I know," I assured her. "I'm not worried."

Just as I turned to walk back into Sugar's room, I noticed my pastor, Mercedes, and Sugar's mother standing by her bedside. I walked closer to the door and saw the doctors unhooking her machines. Immediately, I got excited.

"She's up!" I yelled into the phone as my eyes grew big and my heart started to beat frantically.

"Look at God! Where is the pastor?"

"He's right here." I walked to the door of Sugar's room to say hello and to see Sugar.

My pastor stood over her talking. I assumed they were having a conversation. When I walked into the room fully to get a closer look, I realized my pastor wasn't talking to her—he was reciting the Lord's Prayer. I saw all the wires removed from Sugar's mouth, but she wasn't talking, and her eyes were closed. My heartbeat began to grow sluggish, and I looked around in a state of confusion as I held my phone to my ear. When my pastor finished his prayer and said amen, people began to walk out with their heads down. I stood there confused. My body began to tighten up,

153

my mind began to race, and my hands began to shake as my cellphone fell out of my hands and onto the cold, hard hospital floor. I stared at Sugar's lifeless body, and then I looked up at the ceiling, confused. I'd prayed for four days straight asking God to heal her quickly. I'd asked him to work his miracles and show us all just who had the final say, but God hadn't done anything I'd asked him to do. Sugar wasn't getting up like I'd prayed for. She had died.

I stood there and watched her, hoping this was all a dream or some kind of prank and she'd get up, but she didn't, and she wasn't going to, because she was dead. I began to blink my eyes repeatedly and the room began to spin. I felt nauseous. My legs began to tremble, and I was finding it hard to keep my balance. I would never get to hear her voice again...would never get to see her smile anymore or hear her infectious laugh. We'd planned to be godmothers to each other's children someday, bridesmaids in each other's weddings. Our stories were just beginning, and just like that, her story was over. I couldn't believe it, and everything had happened so fast.

I had just been talking to her, and a few hours later she was on the news. My best friend, my only friend, the only person in this world I loved—probably more than myself—the only person who knew me and loved me for who I was...the person I never went a day without talking to and texting, the person who made living in hell with Mercedes a fun experience...was gone. Just like that. My road dog, my sidekick, my connection with everything that was good in this world was gone forever.

Chapter 27

I stood in that hospital room for over three hours with the same blank stare. People had come in and out screaming and hollering, praying and saying their goodbyes to Sugar, but I just stood there. Casey had passed out. Her mother had to be taken out with a wheelchair and an oxygen tank, and her father went on a warpath throughout the hospital. My pastor cried and kept calm. Mercedes sobbed quietly as she struggled to cater to Casey and make sure she was stable, but she continued to walk right past me without so much as an acknowledgment.

Jordan had come back up to the hospital to see Sugar, and when he found out she'd died, he didn't know what to do with himself. He shook his head and made an attempt to console me, but it didn't work. He hugged me, kissed my cheek, and told me he'd be there until the end, but it didn't help. My stiff body refused to budge or acknowledge his presence, so he walked out. I didn't know what to think and I didn't know what to do. I'd never experienced death. I'd known it would eventually happen to us all, but I'd never thought it would be my best friend. I'd never thought death would happen so soon.

The doctors came in, covered Sugar with a white sheet, and rolled her out en route to the morgue. My eyes followed as I looked on. Knowing it was Sugar under that sheet made me sick to my stomach. I turned around, walked out of the hospital room, and made my way upstairs to the other side where the hotel rooms were. I had no idea what time it was, or when the buses came for me to get back to school. I just wanted to go to sleep. I didn't have a room, but Mercedes had gotten a room with Casey, so I knew there was a place for me to sleep. I walked up to their hotel door and knocked on it. Mercedes opened the door halfway.

"Yes?" she said softly.

"Can I come in and sleep?" I asked. "I'm not sure when the buses run for me to get back to school."

"Casey is in here and I need to be alone with her. She just lost her sister and I want to be here for her. There may be someone who has an extra room, or you can sleep in one of the waiting rooms downstairs in the hospital." She closed the door in my face.

"Wow." I felt stupid, but I wasn't surprised by Mercedes's response at all. I turned around and walked toward the elevator. I glanced at the clock above: it was almost 1 AM. The buses weren't running anymore, and my phone was still on the floor of Sugar's hospital room. I was trapped. I got out of the elevator on the first floor and made my way outside. I figured I'd just walk to the bus station and sit there until the buses started running again. As I turned in the direction of the bus station and began to walk, I bumped right into Jordan.

"I waited out here for hours for you," he said.

"Jordan, what do you want?" I asked impatiently.

"To be here with you. I figured you'd have to come out here sooner or later to catch the bus, so I waited."

"I don't need you to wait, and I don't need you to be here for me."

"Mystery." He hugged me. "Can you *please* listen to me?"

I tried to fight him off, but he refused to let me go.

"Get *off* me," I fussed, trying to force my way out of his arms. The harder I tried, the tighter he hugged me.

"Stop. Just *stop*. Chill out," he demanded. "I don't care how you feel about me anymore. You don't have to be my girlfriend, and you don't have to hear what I have to say about last week. Hell, you don't even have to like me, but I'm *going* to be here for you." Those dark beautiful eyes glared at me. "I'm not gonna let you go through this alone."

Tears burst forth like water from a dam, spilling down my face. I could hear my own sounds, like a distressed child, raw from the inside. I wrestled and wrestled with Jordan to let me go, but it was useless. I wanted to pick up my phone and call Sugar, so I could tell her everything that was happening like I always did, but I couldn't do that anymore, would never be able to again.

I stood outside the University of Pennsylvania hospital, bound by Jordan's firm grip, trying not to lose my mind. His embrace took something out of me that I didn't know I had left to give. I gave up fighting and melted in his arms as I lost my balance and dropped to my knees. Jordan held on to me tightly, dropping to his knees to catch me. I buried my face in his chest and screamed at the top of my lungs. My walls, the walls that held me up and kept me strong, just...*collapsed.* Jordan held on to me in silence, rocking me slowly as tears soaked his jacket.

The pain and agony must've come in waves, minutes of sobbing broken up by short pauses for recovering breaths, before hurling me back into Jordan's outstretched arms of grief. I cried until the room began to spin, and the darkness from outside began to get even darker. The sounds from the outside world suddenly seemed farther and farther away. I didn't know what was going on, but it was peaceful, and I didn't want it to stop. My eyesight blurred, but not because of my tears. Everything became fuzzy, and then I saw nothing at all. My consciousness began to float away, and I could hear my heartbeat pounding ears. Finally, all the feeling in my body drained away until all had gone black.

The next morning, I was awakened by the sound of a dog barking in the background. When I looked around, I realized I was in a bedroom that wasn't mine. There were pictures of athletes everywhere.

"Hey, you're up," said a familiar voice. I turned to my right to see Jordan sitting on the bed next to me. "How do you feel?"

"I don't know." I looked around, confused. "Where are we?"

He chuckled. "We're in my house. You're in my bed. You passed out last night, so I brought you here."

Suddenly, all the memories from the previous night began to come back to me. I immediately realized I wasn't in some horrible nightmare, but it was a reality. I looked down at the oversized t-shirt and basketball shorts I had on.

"I changed your clothes into something more comfortable—and don't worry, I didn't molest you or anything." He chuckled. "I just wanted to help you out."

"It's fine. Thanks." I sat up in the bed and stretched my arms.

"Does your head hurt or anything?"

"A little, I'm good though. I think you should take me back to campus. I shouldn't be in your bed...in your *house*. I don't want to be involved in any more surprise run-ins with your stalker girlfriend."

"You won't have to worry about her ever again. We broke up for good."

"How devastating." I rolled my eyes sarcastically.

"She probably is devastated," he said. "I broke up with *her*."

"I don't know why," I shot back. "*I don't want you.*"

"It's fine, you don't have to want me. I don't want you anymore, either."

I shot him a rude stare and he laughed.

"I'm just kidding. Listen, I can apologize to you a million times and it won't help because in all honesty, I'm not important right now—you are. I was totally wrong for what I did. I wasn't trying to play you for a fool or date two girls at the same time. I've been out of love with Alana for almost a year now, but I didn't know how to tell her that without hurting her. I'd always come up with excuses as to why I couldn't come home for the weekend, why we couldn't go out. It was beginning to get old. She was my college sweetheart, my arm charm, but I'd have never married her. In fact, when I met you, I completely forgot about her. You were that *different* I was looking for...that breath of fresh air that made me realize all women aren't the same. I started to really like you, and I didn't want to tell you about Alana because I knew you'd flip out. My plan backfired in my face. I'm not explaining myself for sympathy or to win you back. We don't have to date, but I still want to be friends. I'll push my feelings to the side just to be close to you and be able to hang out with you again."

I was in the midst of one of the worst experiences of my life, but Jordan still managed to make me smile.

The best thing in the world had been snatched from my life, and I felt alone. There would never be another Sugar. I didn't think I could ever have that kind of connection with anyone else, but having Jordan around gave me some peace of mind.

"We can be friends," I responded softly. "Thanks for being here for me, it really means a lot."

"No problem." He sat next to me. "I can't imagine how you must feel. This is crazy."

"I feel like this life just wasn't made for me to thrive in. Every good thing that's ever happened to me has gone bad."

"That's not true. *Everything* happens for a reason." Jordan wrapped an arm around me. "We'll get through this, and you'll make it. *I promise.*"

"I'm sure with time, everything will get better, but that time won't be for a while. Right now, all I have is me. I can't stand living with Mercedes, but I really don't have a choice. She pays for *everything*, and without her, I'd be on the street. Sugar is gone, so I don't have any more friends. I downgraded from Shippensburg and came to Cheyney to be closer to both of them, and everything just sort of blew up in my face."

"I was like that for a while when my dad died," Jordan reminisced. "I was sixteen at the time and we were really close. Without warning, he had a brain aneurysm, went into a coma, and went brain dead just like Sugar. Everything was so unexpected and happened so fast, I thought I was in a horrible nightmare. We'll get through it, maybe not today or tomorrow, but at some point, you'll be all right. I'm here. I'm not Sugar, but I care."

*****

A week later, Jordan drove me into Philly from school to our church, so we could attend Sugar's funeral. That whole week, I was a wreck. Jordan went back to the hospital and retrieved my phone for me, but it was useless now. I'd only ever used it to talk to Sugar, and not seeing her name pop up or being able to call her left me uninterested in using it. My phone rang off the hook that week, with calls from different people from my church. Sugar's family, and people from other churches who were trying to check on me kept calling, but I didn't answer, and I didn't respond to any text messages. I went to class, and I went back to my room and slept. Jordan came to my room every day to see about me and bring me food, but I didn't really have an appetite. I couldn't concentrate on my studies or I think straight at all, but I did the best I could.

The day of the funeral, Sugar's mother met up with me outside and insisted that I walk in with her family. Casey did a praise dance with the rest of the girls from the church, so she stayed in the back the whole time. I walked up to the casket behind Sugar's mother and sat on the second row with her family. I was so out of it that I didn't remember anything from the actual service except reading her obituary. That was the only piece of Sugar's life that was left, written in words. I couldn't wait to see pictures of us, and some kind of kind message written about our friendship. When I opened the obituary and read it, I saw everyone's name except mine. There were beautiful pictures of Sugar with all of the people who meant the most to her in her life, and there was a very small picture of the two of us all the way at the bottom of the obituary, barely noticeable. It'd been cropped and limited to just our faces.

"This must be a joke," I said to myself.

I read it over twice. I read about how much Sugar adored Mercedes, and how good of a friend, sister, Christian, daughter, and cousin she was to everyone that was important to her, but my name and our friendship was nowhere to be found. I sat there trying to figure out who wrote it, because everyone who knew Sugar knew we were the best of friends.

Finally, Mercedes got up to speak some words of encouragement and told the audience she'd prepared the obituary herself. She looked around the room and smiled, telling all of us she'd prepared it the way Sugar would've wanted it. This woman was officially the devil and bound for hell right along with my mother. I couldn't *believe* her. How could she do such a thing? I put the obituary down and zoned out for the remainder of the service. When it was over, I rode in silence with Jordan to the cemetery.

"I saw that obituary," he said. "Mercedes is seriously evil. I don't think I've ever met someone that heartless."

"Me either." I shook my head. "I can't stay there anymore, and I'm not. I'd rather sleep on the street than in a bed in her home."

"We'll figure something out for you. You need to leave. I wouldn't stay there and be degraded and disrespected like that for health insurance and a cellphone," Jordan sneered.

"I agree." I nodded. "As soon as I can get my things, I'm gone. If you can take me there after we leave here, that'd be great."

"Sure," he replied. We got out of the car and walked up to Sugar's gravesite.

She had a beautiful white coffin that sat on the lowering chamber, waiting to be lowered into the ground. As I approached the casket, I was still in awe that she was really gone. Jordan held my hand as my mind began to think back on all the good times we'd had. I remembered all our laughs and long conversations. I thought back to when I first met her on the baseball field. She was so positive about my situation, and so nice to me. I thought about all the nights we stayed up until daybreak, laughing and joking about life. I thought about the way we texted and talked on the phone all day, every day, never running out of things to say. I thought about how sad I was when I went off to college as I watched her wave goodbye to me from her grandmother's step, and now, my goodbye would be permanent.

As her family and friends surrounded the coffin, the casket-lowering device began to lower Sugar into the ground. My pastor began to pray, and the sobs around me increased. I didn't cry; I was all cried out.

After Sugar's funeral, I moved out of Mercedes's house that same day. When she realized it, she tried making my life a living hell. She cut off my health insurance, my dental insurance, and my cell phone, but I didn't care anymore. I never wanted to see her again. All I had left was a scholarship to finish my education and Jordan.

Chapter 28

I sat in my dorm the next morning looking through my diary, reminiscing about all the memories Sugar and I had shared together. I was supposed to be in class, but I didn't feel like attending. As I sifted through my old memories and dreams, I realized I'd assumed once I got to college, everything in life would come alive for me. I had thought I'd made it. I'd met Sugar and Casey and had a free education. That college acceptance letter to Shippensburg was my golden ticket out of bondage. Looking back, I realized I hadn't really achieved anything.

I was a senior in college at a completely different university. Since I'd switched, my academic scholarship was null and void, so I now had a bunch of student loans. I was still homeless, technically. Sugar was in the ground, and Casey and I couldn't stand each other. At that point in my life, Jordan was the only good thing I had going for me.

As I continued to skim through my diary, a knock sounded at my door. I got up and opened it. A woman from my church named Annette stood there. Everyone referred to her as Aunt Cookie. She was slim, curvy, and stood about five foot four. She had almond-colored skin that always seemed to have just the right amount of makeup on it. She was a seamstress, and a huge fan of creative arts so all of her clothes, heels, jewelry, and hair always stood out. She was fabulous, and probably one of the most hilarious people I'd ever met. She was sweet, very down to earth, and was always my biggest fan since I'd stepped foot in my church some years ago. She knew my life story and had a similar one of her own, so she always rooted for my success. She knew my situation with Mercedes, and after Sugar's funeral, she constantly expressed her worry for my well-being. I was assuming her worry was honest, because she'd made her way across the city on SEPTA and was now standing outside my door with some lady I'd never seen before.

"Hey Aunt Cookie." I cheerfully reached in for a hug.

"Hey pretty girl." She returned the embrace. "It took me three buses to get here, but I'm here. How are you?"

"I'm okay. You didn't have to come all the way up here." I laughed. "You could've just called."

"Well, I actually came up here to meet my girlfriend Sharon. She lives about ten minutes away from here, so she drove me the rest of the way." Aunt Cookie pointed to the other woman. "This is Sharon. Sharon, this is my niece Mystery that I was telling you about."

"Hello," Sharon said. "You're a beautiful girl, I love your name."

"Thank you," I replied. "You guys can come in." I moved out of the doorway and ushered them to my computer chairs to sit down.

"So how are you feeling? I wanted to ensure sure you weren't hanging from the shower rod," Aunt Cookie joked.

"No." I laughed. "I'll be okay, it's just going to take a while."

"And who was that guy you brought to the funeral? He's been to the church a couple of times, too. He's *handsome*."

"That's Jordan." I smiled at her nosey comment. "He's just a good friend, that's all."

"Good friend my behind." She pursed her lips. "Is he single?"

"So he says."

"Oh great, and so are you."

I laughed out loud. "Aunt Cookie, I am *fine*. I do not need a man right now."

"Well if you don't, I'll take him. I need one."

We all burst into laughter.

"I heard you were in need of a new place to stay until graduation in a few months," Sharon said. I immediately looked over at Aunt Cookie, who had a big smile painted on her face. I should've known she was up to something and wasn't just coming all the way down here on the bus just to check on me.

"Listen, Sharon has been my friend for a couple of years now," Aunt Cookie said. "She's awesome, she loves the youth, and she's an evangelist over at Ebenezer Baptist Faith and Deliverance church. She has no man, so she lives alone and not too far from here. I told her about your situation, and she's willing to let you stay with her until graduation."

"And don't worry about any rent money." Sharon smiled. "My door is open just because God laid you on my heart after I heard your touching story."

"I mean, that sounds nice, but—"

"And no, she is not another Mercedes," Aunt Cookie cut me off. "This is my friend, and I know her like the back of my hand. There is nothing fake or fraudulent about her personality. What you see is what you get, so don't be afraid."

"I don't know," I said shyly. "It sounds nice, but...I just don't know."

"Well, where else are you going to sleep? The sidewalk?" Aunt Cookie sounded disappointed.

"Maybe." I shrugged.

I was so tired of moving in with different people. I'd been there and done that for the last ten years. Everyone I'd ever met was never really who they said they were. I'd lived through it and seen it all from my crazy Aunt Carol, a host of others just like her, and vindictive Mercedes. I didn't trust anybody, but yet again, I was at a point where I *really* had no choice. Jordan had offered to let me stay with him and his mom, but that was extremely inappropriate. Besides, I was taking one of Dr. Jackson's classes. Fifty minutes was *enough* of her; I didn't need to go home to her too.

"Listen..." I took a deep breath. "I don't really trust *you*, but I trust Aunt Cookie. I know she'd never put me in harm's way or befriend anybody who could potentially hurt me. Is it all right if I just stay with you on an as-needed basis? Maybe the holiday, or periodically over the summer if I'm not doing an internship?"

"That's perfectly fine," Sharon said. "I'm not forcing you to live with me. You can come and go as you please. My door is open. I'll also add you to my insurance if I can, and I'll make sure you have a working phone in case of an emergency."

"Thank you, that's very nice of you." I smiled.

"No problem. God has blessed me, so I'm willing to be a blessing to others," Sharon affirmed with a head nod. "I only have a one-bedroom apartment, but my bed is big enough for the both of us. If I can help in any other way, just let me know. I'd like for you to come over for dinner tonight, so we can talk and get to know each other a little more. Is that all right?"

"I was actually supposed to be going out to dinner with Jordan," I replied. "Is it okay if I bring him along?"

"No." Sharon shook her head. "I'd really just like to speak to you one-on-one. I know you're uncomfortable about me because of what you've been through, but I really want you to try to bite the bullet and trust God on this one."

Trust God—I'd tried that with Sugar, and it hadn't helped. I certainly still believed God was real, but I didn't consider him to be someone I could trust anymore. However, my life couldn't get any worse, so I had nothing more to lose at that point.

"That's fine, I'll be there," I replied.

"Great." Sharon got up. Aunt Cookie stood up as well.

"I'll be ready for you around seven. Here's my number, and I'll text you the address."

"I'm so proud of you." Aunt Cookie beamed. "Thank you for allowing me to help."

Aunt cookie hugged me and proceeded to walk out of the door with Sharon.

"Thanks, Aunt Cookie." I smiled halfway and walked them to the door. As soon as they were gone, I got on my bed and melted my face into the covers. Over the years, I'd learned to pray for guidance any time a new season began, but *this* time I couldn't bring myself to do it. I felt so empty and dead inside. I couldn't think straight, and I couldn't feel anything.

Chapter 29

Later that afternoon, I sat at the sports bar with Jordan with a rum and coke, watching a hockey game.

"Since when do you drink?" he asked.

"Since today." I took a sip of the bitter drink. "I think this whole weekend merits it."

"You're right, in that case"—he motioned for the bartender's attention— "I'll have what she's having."

"You'll thank me later." I giggled.

"How do you feel about this new woman?"

"I hate the idea, but I'm gonna go through with it anyway. It's only for the weekends when I absolutely need to stay off campus—at least that's what I keep telling myself."

"Man, you're such a strong girl. You have all my respect." He studied me.

"The feeling is mutual," I replied. "I look at your perfect life with your mother, and your status up here...I could only dream of having *half* of your accomplishments. You're an athlete, a frat boy, and you have a mother that loves you and spoils you. Next semester you'll begin law school. That's amazing." I smiled.

"I don't care about that superficial stuff," Jordan said sincerely. "The girls, the athleticism, the status—all that's dead to me now. At this point I just want to succeed. After witnessing an unexpected death like Sugar's, it brought me to the realization that nothing lasts forever. Life can change in a second, and every breath you take is a gift. In the end, I just want to make my mother happy and please the man upstairs."

His ambition was so attractive. I loved hearing Jordan talk about his goals, and his mother. "You'll get it done. Just be grateful you don't have to struggle like I did."

"God gives his toughest battles to his strongest soldiers." He caressed my cheek. "And yes, my parents were very well off. I was blessed. My mom is a highly respected professor, and my pops was a very wealthy number runner." He laughed. "I grew up in the suburbs in a big, single family home where my folks wore matching Rolexes, fancy fur coats, and drove expensive cars. I had an older brother once, but he died when he was four, so I'm an only child. I was spoiled and given the world. My dad was my hero, but just like you, my life hit a turning point."

"Really?" I was surprised.

"Absolutely. Everybody's got a story to tell. When my dad died suddenly, my mother almost lost her mind. She lost her first-born child, and then she lost her husband. That's *tough*. Her entire family and everything she'd built with my dad was snatched from her without warning. Everything I do, I do it for myself, but also for my mother. I want her to look at me and be proud of the man I've become."

"I didn't know she'd lost so much." I took a sip of my drink. "At least she took care of *you*. You were born rich and never knew what it meant to starve. That's something to smile about."

"Why? Because of the money?" He winced. "That's not rich. You aren't rich until you have something money can't buy. The cars, diamonds, expensive furs, and fancy living are only your reward for working your behind off and having something to show for it. My parents' true happiness came from things that couldn't be bought." He smiled. "My parents were so in love. When you saw one, you saw the other. My mother followed him around like she was his shadow. She clung to every word that ever came out of his mouth. He was the *man*. He treated her like a queen and gave her the world. He took care of her like a servant, protected her like a daughter, and worshiped her like she was royalty. My mom always had a sparkle in her eye because of him, and when he died, she did too. His casket stayed in the funeral home for over two weeks because my mother couldn't find it in her heart to bury him. If she could've gotten into the coffin with him, she would have. It was the greatest love story I have ever seen. One day I hope to fall in love like that."

"That is *beautiful*." I sighed. "Sad for her, I'm sure, but beautiful to hear.

"It is." Jordan nodded. "When my heart is really ready to settle down, I'm going to make some woman the happiest woman alive. I'm going to give her everything. I'm gonna work so hard that she never has to unless she wants to. I want children as well. I want to start off with a girl, and then work my way to a boy, maybe even two boys. One dog...and a partridge in a pear tree."

"Sugar and I used to joke around about marrying a rich guy and being swept off our feet like they do in fairytales, but in reality, that would never happen. My future doesn't involve marriage, or snot-nosed kids, or animals, or *pear trees.*" We both laughed.

"Never say never," Jordan warned. "Cupid is coming for you, and when he does, you're going to feel it all in your fingers and your toes. I hope I'm around to tease you about it."

"Maybe." I looked away quickly and gazed at the TV screen in an attempt to regain my composure; Jordan's beautiful aura was throwing me off course. I told him we could *never* be more than friends. I told myself that as well, but the way my hormones exploded every time he looked at me, I thought I'd been lying to the both of us.

Jordan never left my mind; he was always there, mentally if not physically. It was incomprehensible. He was my one stable force, my one point of stability in a world filled with chaos, and I so *desperately* needed him in my life. As we sat in the bar, I began to realize I didn't just like Jordan, I was falling in love with him. The feeling was so strange. It stretched throughout my entire body. It was overwhelming, yet it made me feel complete. It had no bound or length or depth; it was just absolute.

Falling in love with Jordan felt like I was in a dangerous fire, yet I was completely safe at the same time. It felt like peace. I felt as though my heart was dancing around in my chest, and a hole I'd never been aware of before had been filled. Being around him made me feel so light, like I was on top of the world, yet my heart was constricting, and it felt like there was no oxygen in my lungs. It was strange—frightening, even. How I could go from telling him I never wanted to see him again to being completely infatuated by him and wondering how I had *ever* been able to live without him? I sure as hell couldn't imagine being without him now.

Chapter 30

Jordan and I pulled up to Sharon's apartment around 6:15 PM. She lived about ten minutes from Cheyney in a complex just up the road. I stared at the building from the outside in fear, dreading seeing what was on the inside.

"Here we are." Jordan looked at me and chuckled. "You look ecstatic."

"*Very*," I replied sarcastically.

"You know you don't have to go in there, right?" he asked. "You don't have to live with anyone else. If you don't want to come to my house with me and my mom, I can pay for you to stay in a hotel during the holidays."

"No. I hate taking money from you. It feels weird. I know you're just being kind, but it makes me feel needy."

"That's ridiculous. I don't see *needy*. I see a friend who could use some help, and I'd hope if our situations were reversed, you'd do the same for me."

"I would," I replied, "but our roles aren't reversed, so I feel differently about it...I should be fine. What's the worst that can happen?" I opened the car door and got out.

"Alrighty. Call me if you need me, I'll be around." Jordan winked.

"Will do." I closed the car door and he pulled off. Almost immediately, I wished he didn't have to go.

As I walked up to Sharon's apartment building, I looked at the text message she sent me with her apartment number. She was on the second floor. I made my way inside and looked for the stairs. The place wasn't anything special. It looked pretty average and harmless, but I made a mental note of all the emergency exits nearby in case I needed to make a break for it. I waked up the stairs and down the hall toward Sharon's door. When I got to her apartment, I just stood there and stared. I had told myself on the way there that I was all right, but my trembling hands told another story. I wasn't ready to deal with anyone else's demons—not right then, not ever again—but I owed it to Aunt Cookie to at least try.

After five minutes, I finally knocked on Sharon's door and she opened it right away.

"Hey! You made it." She smiled, reaching out to hug me.

"Hi," I responded.

"Come in, take your shoes off. Get cozy. Dinner is ready, I was just waiting on you."

"Cool." I walked in and found the nearest couch to sit down on.

"Do you smell that?" Sharon sniffed the air. "That's the aroma of some of the best cooking you'll ever taste," she jokingly bragged. "Have a look around and make yourself comfortable while I make our plates." The air smelled like mediocre food to me, nothing spectacular, and I didn't want to look around her place or make myself comfortable. I wanted to sit, eat, see what she was all about, and then leave.

"You like barbeque chicken?"

"I do."

"Good because that's what we're having. I made chicken, black-eyed peas, and rice.

I *hated* barbeque chicken, *and* black-eyed peas, but the rice sounded good. I walked around Sharon's dimly lit, gloomy apartment while she made our plates and put them on the table. There weren't many pictures of her family, just her doing church stuff with some of the youth, and a few pictures of a guy who looked to be her son. He was pretty cute actually, and he appeared to be around my age. I walked back into the living room and sat down at her dinner table.

"How have things been since the funeral? Everything coming along okay?"

I knew she'd bring that up. I really wasn't in the mood to talk about Sugar's funeral, or my feelings about it. Everyone from my church had been calling me nonstop since the day before to talk about it, and I'd ignored every last one of them. But, considering Sharon was right in front of my face, there was no getting around it.

"I feel okay, as okay as I can be considering the circumstance."

"You know, I was in your shoes once." She brought my plate of food to me and went back into the kitchen to get hers.

"Good. So you should know how it feels to walk in them and not really want to talk about it." I rolled my eyes.

"I sure do. You know, I have a son who'll be thirty next year." She sat down at the dinner table. "When

I first got pregnant with him, I asked God for a little girl every day. When I was little, I dreamed about having a daughter. I never wanted a son, but God insisted that I have one. So after I had Ernest, my husband and I tried getting pregnant again. It took us three years, but I finally got pregnant again, and to God be the glory, it was a *girl*. The moment I found out was probably one of the happiest memories of my life. I was on cloud nine and couldn't *wait* to give birth. I had a big baby shower, and I fixed up her nursery. The first time I held her in my arms I was in heaven. When she was about three months old, I took her to my mother's house with me for a quick second. My mother ran a daycare out of her home so when I went in, I put her upstairs in the bassinet away from the kids. Unfortunately, two kids snuck into the room and were tossing a football back and forth. One of them lunged for the ball and flew into my daughter's bassinet, causing her to fly out of it and hit her head on the nightstand nearby. We all panicked and rushed her to the hospital, but it was too late. She was declared brain dead by the doctors, and I lost her."

My heart instantly broke for Sharon as I listened to her story. I supposed she really did know what I was going through.

"I have *never* experienced pain like that in my life," she continued. "To this day, I still haven't. To lose a child, especially one I prayed for, will leave a permanent scar for the rest of my life. After I lost Michele, I had the whole city come to my rescue— at least that's what it felt like. Every time I turned around there were people at my door with baskets, food, flowers, and cards. People were calling me and asking invasive questions. It was *very* annoying. While it's a nice gesture to ask and extend a helping hand to others after they experience death, it's impossible for them to truly understand it unless they've walked a mile in your shoes. After they asked me so many times, I grew disconnected from people."

"That's *exactly* how I feel." It felt so good to listen to someone who could relate. "I hate when people ask me questions almost as much as I hate them telling me *I know how you feel*, and *It'll be okay.*"

"Understood." Sharon nodded. "Take it from someone who's been there before: I don't know how *you* feel, but know how *it* feels, and I'll be here for you as much as you will allow me to be."

"Thanks." I smiled and forced myself to take another spoonful of her nasty food.

Sharon's encouragement led me to believe her care was genuine. I felt so misunderstood by everyone, and she seemed to be the only one who could feel my pain. It felt nice.

"I've also been down your road of betrayal before," she said. "We have a lot more in common than you think."

"Really?" I asked.

She chuckled. "A couple years ago, after I became an evangelist, I began to get interested in helping the youth at my church. A good amount of the young girls there were poor and came from underprivileged families who didn't believe in them and ignored them, and I developed a special place in my heart to mentor them. On the weekends I would allow them to come over to my house that I shared with one of my friends. I would take them out, buy them clothes, feed them, and spend time with them. One of the girls I mentored was a troublemaker, however, and was constantly causing confusion amongst the rest of the girls. After a while I got fed up and told her she couldn't come over anymore until she got her act together. She got angry and rebellious and decided to write up a letter to the bishop, accusing me of being a lesbian, and she said I was sleeping with the friend I shared the house with. She got the other girls to sign it, saying they were afraid to be in my home because they felt like I would eventually make a pass at them. When the letter got to the bishop, I was forced to step down from my ministry with the youth."

As she told me the story, I saw pain and tears flow from her eyes. She seemed very hurt. I felt so bad for her.

"I have a heart for young people, and all I tried to do was help those girls, but they all turned on me and humiliated me. It's okay though, because God doesn't like ugly, and you reap what you sow. They'll get what's coming to them." She wiped her eyes and continued to eat.

My heart ached for her, because I knew how it felt to be double-crossed and made to look like a monster by people you trusted or confided in. Maybe we really did have more in common than I thought.

"That's a shame," I said. "I'm sorry you had to go through that, but in the end, it made you stronger, and you're able to tell your story and encourage someone like me who needed to hear it."

"I agree," she said. "I never stopped wanting to help young people, and I'm glad, because I felt led to help you."

"This food is good," I lied. "But I'm a little full, and my menstrual cramps are starting to bother me." I got up from the table and went over to my purse.

"You get bad cramps too?" she asked.

"Severe...especially on the first day. I always take Percocet for them" I pulled out my meds and popped one in my mouth. I walked over to the table and took a sip of my juice to wash it down.

"I get them too," she said. "I always use a heating pad to help soothe them. You can go lie in my bed and take a nap if you want. I'll give you my heating pad until they ease up."

"That'd be great."

I hated my menstrual cycle. It always came on at the most inopportune time and caused me the worst pain. I thought about calling Jordan to come get me, but I was in pain and just wanted to lie down somewhere until the Percocet kicked in. Sharon showed me to her room and gave me her heating pad. She closed her bedroom door and left me to myself. I fell asleep almost before my head hit the pillow.

I was awakened almost five hours later by someone's hand under my shirt, touching one of my breasts. I struggled to open my eyes, and when I did, I saw a female arm in the dark that was attached to the hand under my shirt. I wasn't sure if I was hallucinating from the medicine, or if I was dreaming. I quickly jerked away, changed positions, and lay on my stomach. When I moved, the hand moved quickly. My heart began to race, and I lay there trying to wake up and gather my thoughts to figure out what had just happened.

Did this woman just touch me? I thought. *I know she didn't just touch me. Am I tripping? No. I know I just felt someone touching me. I'm not crazy, and I know for sure that was* not *a dream.*

My mind went in circles for about ten minutes, and once I was able to accept what had just taken place, I felt extremely uncomfortable...and pissed.

What the hell? My thoughts and my heart raced. The entire time I had thought this woman was nice, sweet, and wanted a daughter to replace the one she lost. I'd just met her, and she'd wasted absolutely NO time showing me who she really was

I lay there, waiting for the right time to get up and run for it. *I knew there was a reason I remembered where those emergency exits were.* My purse was in the living room, so I couldn't reach for it to call Jordan. I was so afraid to get up and walk into the other room. The whole time, she didn't move a muscle. I wasn't sure if she thought I was asleep, or if I was even aware of what she was unsuccessful at trying to do. I stared out the window next to the bed for almost 45 minutes, upset, uncomfortable, and afraid. Eventually, she eased out of the bed and went into the bathroom. As soon as I heard the bathroom door close, I got up and ran for my life.

I grabbed my purse, pulled out my phone, grabbed my sneakers, and hurried out of the house. I raced down the emergency exit as fast as I could with tears running down my face. I'd almost let my guard down and opened my heart once again, and just like the previous times, I had been betrayed and manipulated. *This* time, however, would be the *last* time. I was sick and tired of all of these people. That night I made a vow to myself that I was done living with people. I was so disgusted and angry at the world that I would've slept with stray dogs on the *street* before I ever slept in a bed in someone else's home again.

Chapter 31

Two months later

I sat on the side of the bed at the Grand Floridian Resort in Orlando, Florida, waiting for Jordan to finish dressing so we could go to dinner. During his downtime he played on a semi-pro football team, and their national tournament was in Florida this year. I wasn't really a fan of football, or flying on an airplane, but I was a fan of Jordan. Anywhere he was, I wanted to be there too. I was also happy to be away from school. College graduation was a week away, and I'd been studying my behind off for finals. I was tired of reading textbooks, memorizing formulas, and practically living out of the library, so the temporary change of scenery was welcomed.

I didn't quite have a plan figured out for post-graduation yet, but as long as it didn't involve living in anyone else's house or meeting any more so-called mentors, I was content with going with the flow of things. Sharon had been the straw that broke the camel's back. I was *so* over it after her. To add salt to the wound, she'd lied to Aunt Cookie about what happened that night. She told her she cooked a bunch of food and I never showed up. Aunt Cookie called me crying, talking about how disappointed she was in me, and how embarrassed I made her. I didn't bother to defend myself and tell her what *really* happened. I didn't care enough. I did tell

Jordan, though, and he was *pissed*. He wanted to say something to Sharon, but I told him to leave it alone.

After twenty minutes, Jordan emerged from the bathroom, adjusting his tie. He was so gorgeous in his gray pin-striped suit, I *swore* I was drooling. How had I gotten so lucky? How long would I continue to play the friend card, knowing what my heart really wanted? Jordan had the kind of face that could stop a woman right in her tracks. There was no one feature that made him so handsome, but his eyes came close. From them emanated an intensity, an honesty, and a gentleness.

"You look beautiful." He looked at me and smiled. I wore a little black dress that hugged my curves and stopped a little above my knees.

"Me?" "I feel pretty plain in this dress. I would've packed differently if I'd known *Disney World* and *five-star restaurants* were part of our agenda."

"You're graduating college in a few days. Certainly, you didn't think I would drag you to Florida and not have some sort of surprise up my sleeve." He winked. I shook my head and stood up to give myself a once-over in the mirror before we left.

A few months before, Jordan and I had a conversation about all the many times his mother had taken him to Disney. He talked about it being the most magical place on earth while I sat there trying to live vicariously through his memories. All my life I'd wanted to go to Disney World. The commercials on TV made it look like a fairytale vacation, but I lived a childhood that told a *different* tale, one that didn't involve fairytales, Mickey Mouse, and magical pixie dust. I told Jordan that the very first time I could afford a vacation, I would spend it in Disney World. While there was an entire planet's worth of art, architecture, and culture to discover, I found so much value in cultivating a more carefree, innocent self. I had been robbed of it during my younger days, and I wanted to relive as much of it as I could.

Entering Disney World was like entering a world of illusion made possible by the company's unparalleled attention to detail. It really was as magical as they said. Every area had a history, from the iconic Cinderella castle to Typhoon Lagoon, a surf pool supposedly created by a make-believe storm. Then there was Big Thunder Mountain, the fictional former center of an 1850s gold-mining operation.

The company also made shrewd use of background music; merry soundtracks played just at the threshold of my consciousness nearly everywhere we went. Disney even lent a homey feel to the Main Street, USA, area of the Magic Kingdom by pumping out the aroma of freshly baked cookies. The minute we stepped into the Magic Kingdom, it was bathed in an ethereal golden glow. There were barbers at the Harmony Barber Shop who stood ready. They really did cut hair too, and there was a barbershop quartet to go along with it. As the days went by, I became more and more distracted by trying to separate the genuine from the counterfeit.

For dinner on our first evening, Jordan and I walked from the Yacht Club to the shops and restaurants along Disney's Boardwalk, where the atmosphere is 1920s Atlantic City—bare light bulbs, street performers, and a wooden walkway that ran along the lake. Then there was the bar at Stormalong Bay that was pleasant and civilized, populated by attractive people in business attire who sat at tables and worked on their laptops; they were either there for a corporate event or they were cast members portraying people there for a corporate event. The sophisticated adult in me was pleased, and my inner child was ready for another fun-filled evening with Jordan.

"This is the best surprise ever. You win. No one has *ever* done anything like this for me before." I walked over and hugged him. *I shouldn't have done that.* As he pulled me close and hugged me back, I puckered my lips, subconsciously leaning in for a kiss. Just before my lips touched his, I recoiled in shock. Jordan's usually playful smile had drawn into a cocksure grin.

"Whoa." He let go of me and backed up. "Where did that come from, *friend?*"

"I...I'm sorry." I looked away, completely embarrassed. "It was just a reaction to—" Jordan looked at me, amused at my being disheveled. His hand reached for mine and they interlocked. He moved into my personal space and did what I'd been wanting to do for the last three months. He kissed me—tentatively at first, passionately, then tenderly. His body was warm and toned as he wrapped his arms around me, his touch so comforting. His voice was exotically deep with a serious tone as his lips broke away from mine and brushed against my ear.

"I love you." I looked back at him with a nonchalant gaze and a weak smile. Of course, the blush that accompanied it was a dead giveaway that

I loved him too. I'd never heard those words before. Butterflies fluttered around in my stomach, and my nerves were completely shot to hell.

"I love you too," I choked out. *Is this really happening to me?*

"I love you because of who you are." He cupped my face in his hands. "You are the most amazing woman I have ever met in my life. You made it to college on a scholarship and a prayer. You never gave up." He lifted up my forearms. They were cut up and permanently scarred from knives and razor blades. "I see a lot of battle scars," he continued, "but I also see a reminder that the battle is not over. No weapons formed against you have ever prospered, and they never will. You've gone through so much disappointment in your life. Dreams were deferred, promises were broken, and so much adversity happened, but you still wake up every day expecting something good to happen. You give me hope, and you give me chills." Jordan looked at me like I was a goddess.

Tears filled my eyes and fell from my face. "I always say there are people in our lives who are here for a season, and there are people in our lives who are here for a reason. My life has been rough because I've spent so much time giving seasonal things lifetime expectations. I've always just wanted to find home like everyone else, but God had a journey in mind. Throughout my journey, I've encountered a lot of crisis, but in that crisis, I met Christ. I used to look at my life and regret having suffered so much, but if you take away my crisis, you take away my anointing." I smiled, wiping my tears. "All the ugly and uncomfortable things I've endured have shaped and molded me to touch hearts and win souls for the kingdom of God in a way only experience could've prepared me for, and it is because of my pain that I can appreciate this moment. I've always believed that everything in life has an opposite. To everything in life there is a season. This season is for love."

Jordan openly gazed at me, his dark eyes making me weak in the knees. He had the heart of a lion and the soul of an angel. He pushed me against the wall and kissed me like he could eat me alive, and I had the silverware and napkin, ready to be devoured. *So long, Christian Grey.* As the sun set over the crystalline sky in room 2305, Jordan Jackson showed me 50 shades of Disney.

Chapter 32

The day had come when I would officially become a college graduate. I'd waited my entire life for this moment of truth, and there it was staring me in the face. I looked around my empty room at all of my things packed into boxes and bins. It reminded me of the first day my grandparents had dropped me off at Shippensburg University. When I'd looked around for the first time, I'd seen an empty dorm room full of possibilities. Four years later, all of them had been fulfilled. I came. I saw. I conquered. I left my mark, I told my story, and I completed a journey that many people after me would need a map to. I utilized my stumbling blocks as stepping stones. *I was living proof that whatever God ordered, he paid for.*

As I put on my gown, there was a knock at my door. I so badly wished it were Jordan, but he had a job interview and apologized for not being able to make it. I opened my door and smiled as Sugar and Casey's mother graced my presence. She pulled me into the biggest hug and extended the brightest smile ever.

"Hey," I said excitedly. "I didn't know you were really gonna come."

"You look so pretty." She let go of me, so she could stare me down. "I wouldn't have missed this for the world. I'm *so* proud of you."

Seeing her in front of me was very bittersweet. She was the spitting image of Sugar. It bought tears to my eyes because Sugar used to talk about the day I'd finally graduate college. *"I'm going to be the loudest one on the quad, screaming for you and acting like an idiot."* I really missed her, but having her mother there meant the world to me.

"Are you by yourself?" I asked as she walked in and closed my door.

"Yes. I left at 8 this morning trying to find the bus route to get here. I didn't know where I was going, and I dropped my phone in water last night, so I couldn't call anyone...but I was coming no matter what. Sugar would be so proud of you right now."

"She would." I bit my lip and nodded to keep from tearing up.

"Mystery...I know you haven't known me very long, but I've known you since the day you met Sugar. You were a blessing to my daughter, and it is an honor to know you. I'm so proud to be in your presence, and I'm so proud that my daughter touched your life and impacted you to love and trust." She let go of me and reached for my graduation cap on my dresser. "Come-on, let's go graduate."

A tear fell from my eye and I wiped it quickly.

"I'm ready." I smiled. "Let's do it."

Toni and I walked outside and separated. She went to find a seat and I joined the rest of my graduating class in line. As we began to walk through the hundreds of people gathered under the tent to greet us, I noticed my family members among the crowd. I saw both of my grandmothers standing proud, and my aunts and cousins were in attendance as well.

When my name was called, I made my way across the stage to receive my degree, crossing the threshold of adolescence into adulthood. That walk I took was my walk out of the wilderness. That walk closed the chapter in my life that made me feel like an underachiever. It quieted the voices in my head that told me I belonged in a psychiatric ward instead of a university. It challenged every finger pointed at me that made me feel like everything that ever went wrong in my life was because of me. *I did it.* I received my diploma and proceeded down the other side into my new season. When I made it down the last step, I saw Jordan standing in the grass watching me. As soon as I saw him, I ran up to him with opened arms.

"Congratulations, baby." He kissed me. "This is only the beginning."

"I thought you weren't coming, liar." I nudged him playfully.

"There you go again, underestimating me." He winked. Under a tent full of screaming families and smiling faces, his smile screamed the loudest. It's a scientific fact that after so many storms, a rainbow will eventually appear. Jordan was my rainbow, and I wondered if there really was a pot of gold at the end of him.

Chapter 33

That summer, Jordan and I spent every waking moment together. He moved all my things into his basement for storage and gave me the keys to his mother's penthouse that she owned in the center of the city. She often used it for her guests that flew into town for her meetings and business lunches, but she was vacationing in Paris for the summer, so Jordan allowed me to stay there.

He obtained an internship working for the Dow Jones and if all went well, he'd be hired as a salaried employee at the end of it. Being with Jordan reminded me a lot of the good old days Sugar and I used to have. He took me on all kinds of road trips with his football team, out to fancy restaurants, and vacations along the beach. Although I'd given him my virginity already, as well as a few other special moments, he still respected my privacy and never spent the night with me. We'd hang out, laugh, and watch movies, and then he'd go back home and call me, then we'd spend the rest of the night talking on the phone. Every time I needed clothes or money, he was always right there to give me whatever I needed. I loved him so much, and it felt so good.

I sat in the library downtown one Tuesday afternoon, writing essays and applying to grad schools. Jordan always told me I was too gifted for life's mediocrity that many people sometimes settled into after college. *"I don't see you stopping at a bachelor's degree in psychology. I see you as a Doctor of Psychology. I see you changing lives and making an impact."* I took his advice and decided to apply to a master's program.

"Hey you," Jordan whispered softly as he walked up behind me and sat down next to me.

"Hey." I was slightly surprised. "I thought you were working."

"I was. They gave us a two-hour lunch today, so I decided to come see what you were up to. How are the essays coming?"

"I've applied to the University of Penn, Temple, Drexel, and Cheyney's graduate psych program. I've completed the essays for all of them except UPenn. They require it to be five thousand words."

"Holy cow." He raised an eyebrow. "I don't even think I have five thousand words in my vocabulary."

"Me either." I laughed.

A woman sitting next to us stopped typing and shot us an irritated glance.

"I'm sorry, I'm too loud," Jordan whispered. The woman shook her head and went back to typing.

"Sorry." I looked at her and felt bad for interrupting.

"Come take a break." Jordan looked back at me. "There's a new pizza place up the street I want to try."

"I haven't really had an appetite. I'm still trying to get over this stomach virus."

"It's still bothering you?"

"A little. It's getting better, but I don't think pizza would help at the moment. You go ahead. I'll grab a salad or something later."

"Cool. Well I'm off at five. You want to do something later on? How about bowling?"

"I think I'm just gonna finish this up and go back to the apartment and relax for the day. I don't really feel up to the noisy environment and the walking."

Jordan sighed, irritated. "Fine, I'll go by myself."

"You can always come over and relax with me." I smirked and pinched his cheek. "I'm sure we can find *something* to do."

"No thanks. It's a nice summer day, I don't want to be in the *house*." He rolled his eyes.

"What's with the attitude?" I winced.

"You. You've been like this for the past couple weeks. You don't want to go to the gym, you don't want to go to the movies, and you don't want to go out to eat. I'm surprised you even came to the library. What is *up* with you? You've gotten so boring."

"*Boring?*"

The woman next to us began to type loudly, expressing her growing frustration.

"Yes, *boring*," Jordan shot back. "We have so much time on our hands, and you get lazy all of a sudden."

"Oh great, now I'm *lazy*, too?" I flung my hands in the air. "Have a good day, Jordan. I'm going to finish my essays now."

"And you don't even *care*." He shook his head in disgust.

"No, *I don't*. I just told you I've been under the weather, and you're being selfish about it."

"Whatever, you've been under the *so-called* weather for a week, and the week before that you claimed to be tired. I'm not buying that, you're just lazy."

"Can you *stop* with the name-calling?" My voice elevated

"No, I can't. If it's okay for you to call me selfish then it's okay for me to call you what you are—*lazy*."

The more he talked, the angrier I became. "Jordan, get the *hell* away from me. *Please*."

"No problem." He immediately stood up and stormed out of the library as fast as he could.

I couldn't *stand* when he acted like the world revolved around him, and then to call me lazy and spoiled? I was so upset. I didn't feel like being in the library anymore. I was ready to go home. I gathered my papers and quickly stuffed them in my bag.

"I swear, can you *get* any louder?" The woman sitting next to me said sharply.

"Not now lady," I responded. "I have an attitude." I was in the mood to slap somebody, and if she didn't leave me alone, it would end up being her.

"I don't care about your little attitude. You've ignored mine for the past fifteen minutes."

"I *said* I was sorry."

"Sorry means it won't happen again. You and your little Hershey kiss over there have been working my nerves again, and again, and again."

"That little Hershey Kiss has a *name*," I snapped.

"I have a name too, but you didn't bother asking me for it before you referred to me as *lady*."

This woman was really starting to piss me off.

"I apologize," I stated calmly, making a final attempt at keeping the peace. "What's your name?"

"That's more like it. I'm Jewel." She smiled and stuck her hand out for me to shake. "What's yours?"

"Mystery," I mumbled.

"Well you *certainly* aren't mysterious about your rude behavior or your tone of voice in this library."

I shot up out of my chair like lightning and got in her face. "You know what—"

"*And,*" she cut me off, unmoved by my anger. "There's nothing mysterious about your nasty attitude either. Your feelings and emotions are all over your face. You're a pretty girl with a pretty name—you should act like it," she said calmly.

"What is with everybody *judging* me today?" I grabbed my bag. "It's like you people have no filter."

"Neither do you. You sat in that chair for a half hour and talked loudly, not caring that this is a library or that you were being disruptive. Then you pissed off Prince Puddin' Pop with your selfish ways before accusing *him* of being selfish."

"First of all, you have *no* right minding my business, because I didn't—"

"*Sit down girl,*" she said firmly, cutting me off again. "I wasn't minding your business. You were loud enough for the entire library to hear." She laughed. "You should treat people how you want to be treated." The woman's infectious personality caused my temper to simmer down. Jewel was right—I was extremely emotional over something so insignificant.

"Listen, I apologize." I sat back down and began to calm down. "I didn't mean to be loud on purpose. I got upset with Jordan because I despise being called names. This is my first time in a relationship. It's my first time with love, period."

"Well welcome to the battlefield of love." She laughed. "This is only the beginning. A word of advice from someone who's been married for thirty years: pick your battles. Trust me, there will be plenty to choose from."

"I'm not usually this short fused with him," I explained, "but I'm human I guess. I'll apologize later."

"How much do you love him?" she asked.

"I love him a lot." My eyes lit up. "We just haven't been on the same page lately and I'm not sure why."

"I think I have the answer," she replied with a twinkle in her eye.

"What's that?"

"I want you to get up and go next door into that CVS. When you go in there, go to aisle six, and look to your left. Buy what you see and come back and see me."

"Really? You're going to send me on a scavenger hunt?" I began to get irritated again.

"Trust me." She winked.

I got up from my seat and sighed as I walked out of the library. I walked next door into the CVS and made my way to aisle six, muttering obscenities along the way.

"I swear...today is just *not* my day. It's time for me to go back to the apartment and take a—"

I froze as I stopped in the aisle and turned to my left. Standing in front of me were five different pregnancy tests.

Chapter 34

"Shut the *front* door!" I stared at the boxes. "No way can I be pregnant."

Suddenly, it hit me. I'd missed my period the previous month. Come to think of it, I'd missed it the month before as well. I pulled out my phone and looked at my calendar. It was set to come on the 8th of the month. I checked the date, and it was the 17th. *I didn't get it this month either.*

"Oh...my...God." I didn't have a stomach virus, and I wasn't just moody and exhausted for no apparent reason. I was *pregnant*. I purchased three pregnancy tests and took them right in the store's restroom. Almost harmoniously, the spaces on all six of the sticks began to spell out *PREGNANT*.

As I watched the letters appear, I swore my heart stopped. I slid down the wall onto my knees. I'd said I was content with going with the flow of things after graduation, but I hadn't meant *this* kind of flow.

Was I really equipped to be someone's mother? I'd never had the chance to have a good mother myself. I didn't have a job, or an income. I'd just finished applying to all of those grad schools. I supposed I could kiss a continuing education goodbye.

"This can't be happening to me." Tears welled up in my eyes.

The bathroom door opened slowly, and I'd almost forgotten it was a public bathroom. I quickly wiped my eyes and stood up to grab the pregnancy tests off the sink. As the door opened, Jewel emerged in the doorway with a smile on her face.

"Hello there," she said. "I figured I'd find you in here."

As soon as I saw her, I had so many questions. "How could you tell I was pregnant? You don't even know me."

Jewel laughed and walked into the bathroom with me. "I've been in this world forty-eight years, sweetheart, and I have three children all around your age. There isn't too much a mother doesn't know."

"But how?" I asked.

"Instinct. Intuition. I heard you talking about a stomach virus, and I could see by the way Mr. Dark Chocolate had you all hot and bothered that it was hormones. Congratulations." She smiled.

"Congratulations?" I looked at her like she was crazy. "I'm not ready to be a mother."

"Well ready or not, welcome to motherhood," Jewel said. "This is life, honey. It never happens the way *we* want it to, it happens the way *God* wants it to."

"I'm so confused...I *just* graduated college. I was supposed to be gearing up for grad school, and now." I looked at the tests one more time. "I'm not sure what I'm gonna do now."

"You sound a lot like me when I was your age. I got pregnant right out of college too."

"And what did you do?"

"Here." She pulled out a piece of paper and gave me her phone number. "Give me a call when you've settled down. We'll talk."

Placing the pregnancy tests and Jewel's number in my purse, I headed out the bathroom door.

"And by the way." I turned around at the sound of her voice. "Don't miss your blessing because it comes in a package that looks different from the one you ordered."

Briefly, I stood there and took in her words before proceeding out of the store.

"I still can't believe this," I said to myself. "I've got to go find Jordan."

I walked at a fast pace up the road toward the pizza shop where he said he wanted to eat lunch. What would his reaction be? Would he be happy? Would be he upset? Scared? Angry? *Maybe I should get an abortion. I'm not ready to be someone else's mother just yet.*

What would Jordan's *mother* say? She would have a fit. She would blame me for ruining his life and talk about me like a dog. Something told me I should've kept my virginity until I got married. My grandmother always said forehead kisses were how men absorbed all the sense in your brain. I should've taken heed and stayed woke.

Just as I approached the pizza shop, I noticed Jordan sitting by the window. He had no idea his life was about to change. Just as I grabbed the door handle, I froze. Jordan sat at the table with his ex, Alana. They were laughing, joking, and eating pizza.

Chapter 35

I sat in the penthouse later on that evening crying my eyes out, staring at my phone. I'd called, and texted Jordan a dozen times and he'd ignored all of them. I knew he was home, and I knew he was getting my phone calls and texts. I didn't understand what was going on. There had to be some kind of explanation for this. I was so in love with him. Had he really just done this to me a second time?

Jordan, where are you? I decided to text again. After about five minutes, he finally responded.

Working late. I'll hit you up sometime tomorrow.

My eyes grew big and my mouth dropped open.

Working late? Yeah right. I picked up my phone and called him. I was pregnant with his baby, and he was eating lunch with his ex. Both of us had some explaining to do, and we were gonna do it *today*. If I had to blow his phone up all night long, I was prepared to. After the fifth ring, he finally answered.

"What's up?" He sounded annoyed.

"I've been calling and texting you *all* afternoon. You're really going to be a jerk and ignore me like this over some stupid misunderstanding we had earlier?"

"I wasn't ignoring you. I told you I was working late, and I'd hit you up tomorrow."

"Right, because earlier you were excited to hang out after work and now all of a sudden you have to work late?"

"Yup."

"*Jordan.*" I felt myself getting even more irritated. "What's going on? I came to the pizza shop to join you for lunch, but I saw you already had company."

There was dead silence on the other end of the phone.

"Hello?" I said.

"I'm here," he replied. There wasn't an ounce of pity in his voice.

"You have *nothing* to say for yourself?" I asked.

"No, I don't actually."

I was at a complete loss for words. What'd gotten into him?

"You know what, we need to talk," he said. "Today's events really had me thinking about our relationship on a long-term level. This boyfriend-girlfriend situation isn't going to work out anymore."

I felt my heart do a free fall into my lap. *Did he just dump me?*

"Are you serious?" My voice shook.

"I'm sorry to have strung you along like this. There's a lot about me you don't know and wouldn't understand. This just isn't going to work. I'm sorry." He spoke to me like I was a stranger.

"Jordan," I pleaded. "What is—"

"I have to go. I'll hit you up tomorrow." The line went dead, as did my soul. I thumped onto the chair and began to cry. My sobs punched through, ripping through my muscles, bones, and guts. I felt my heart yanking in and out of my chest as the muscles of my chin trembled like a small child. I looked toward the window, hoping the light could soothe me, but it didn't. I couldn't speak, couldn't breathe, nothing.

The world around me became a blur of color that melted to gray. I cried for nearly an hour before anger started to set in. What had Alana said to him? Why couldn't she just leave him alone—leave *us* alone. I'd stayed out of it the last time because I was new to love, but now I was a pro. Come hell or high water, somebody owed me an explanation.

I got up from the chair I was sitting in and put my sandals on. I stormed out of the apartment and raced down the stairs.

"I'm going to kill that girl," I said out loud. "I'm going to strangle *her*, and I'm going to shoot *him*."

I rushed down the steps of the large apartment building and out the door. When I got outside, there was Jordan, standing below the steps, looking directly at me. I stopped dead in my tracks as we locked eyes, mine still red and puffy from crying.

"Can I come up? Can we talk upstairs?" he asked.

"No. *Hell no*. We're going to talk right here, right now. What is all this about?"

He walked up the steps and sat down with his back turned toward me.

"Just sit down beside me please," he said calmly.

"Jordan, I—"

"Mystery, please? Sit down. For real."

"No," I shouted. "The man I knew would've *kicked* your ass all over this place for breaking my heart like this." Tears began to flow from my eyes again. "You told me you *loved* me, you told me I was different, you told me I *meant* something to you. What the hell happened in the course of a couple hours?"

"Mystery." He refused to look at me. "Come sit down next to me so we can have a civilized conversation."

"NO!" I continued to shout at the back of his head since he refused to stand up and face me like a man. "I believed you, I listened to you, and I changed who I was for *you*," I cried. "Look at me when I'm screaming at you!" I demanded. I walked down the steps and stepped in front of him, so he could see my face. "How could you *lie* to me like—" My entire body froze. It was more than just a slight tingle running underneath my skin; it was as if someone had attached a live wire to each of my nerves. In Jordan's hands was a black jewelry box with a 2-carat diamond ring sitting inside of it.

"You underestimate me again, psych major." He stood up and grinned. I wanted to speak, but I couldn't. My mind was unable to comprehend or process the image it was being sent by my eyes. I looked away, then looked back to see if it was still there. It was. "Alana is a manager at Tiffany's. She's happily engaged and wants nothing to do with me other than helping me pick out the most expensive ring to get the commission from it. I dumped you as my girlfriend because I want you as my wife." He walked up to me and wiped away my excess tears.

"Oh my God." My voice shook as more tears fell from my face. "You scared me. I thought you didn't love me anymore."

"Our love is evergreen baby—it'll never die." He kissed me. "I don't want anyone else but you. You are the one I was born to love, to trust, to save, and to nurture to full health. I see who you really are. I see right to your core and I still love you without reserve." He got down on one knee. "Will you marry me?"

"I will marry you," I replied. He barely placed the ring on my finger before I jumped into his arms and wrapped my arms around his neck, hanging on for dear life. "In this journey, I have tried every path and pushed on every door. You are living proof that love is real. To be in your company is a little slice of heaven that I would love to indulge in for the rest of my life. I love you."

"It's me and you, forever. Just the two of us. We're gonna change the world." He kissed my cheek.

"You mean the three of us?" I broke free from his hug and gazed at back at him.

"Three?"

I took his hand and placed it on my belly. "Three. We're gonna have a baby. *I'm pregnant.*"

Jordan fainted on the steps.

The End...

Epilogue

Jordan and Mystery went on to live a fairytale that God hand-selected and predestined just for them. They were married on a beautiful beach in Mexico and welcomed a baby boy into the world a short time later. As the years progressed, they went on to welcome two more children, a girl, and another boy. As their love story continues to be written, who knows—maybe there's room for a few more.

Jordan became a successful private banker, and Mystery loved psychology so much, she earned a PhD in it. Sooner than later she hopes to become a psychology professor at a four year institution.

Mystery has never seen or spoken to her mother again-and it wasn't because she didn't want too. She loved her mother enough to reach out over the years to fix things, but her mother refused, eventually disappearing to Arizona for good. She changed her phone number, blocked Mystery from all of her social media accounts, and was never seen or heard from again. But her mother's abrupt ending wasn't really an ending at all. The road that is recovery from a childhood without a mother's love, support, and attunement was long and complicated.

Mystery's life had only just begun, and there was so much her mother missed. She missed her daughter's middle school, high school, college, and grad school graduations. She missed prom send offs, and milestone birthday parties, she wasn't there to see her fall in love for the first time, she missed her engagement party, her wedding, and the births of all her children. Mystery could never inquire about her family history, medical questions, or how to navigate life's questions.

A mother's relationship with her daughter forms the primary foundation for how she formulates her sense of self. It acts as the basic template for her understanding of how relationships work in the world. Mystery walked through life with a hole in her heart for a very long time. She had a hard time forming close friendships, healthy boundaries, learning true love, and understanding herself as a person. For years, Mystery internalized her mother's words and actions and, long after childhood, she sought out other relationships—with friends and lovers alike—that echoed her maternal one, no matter how much pain it caused. Every relationship she formed while in her teens and twenties was all about her mother, filling the empty space in her heart with the same kind of cruelty and uncaring.

As a degreed, intellectual professional, Mystery understood all the dynamics on an intellectual level, but it was a long road to owning it on an emotional level because of the damage the past had done to her spirit. She spent years in therapy trying to get her mother's voice out of her head- the voice that told her she was too fat as a teenager, the voice that tells her today that she's a lousy housekeeper, a bad mother, a horrible wife, and the one that sends a staunch reminder that nothing about her or her life will ever be good enough. Therapy worked eventually, but to this day, the old wounds still bleed when she's fatigued.

Life happened, still, God favored her. He smiled on her marriage and blessed her womb. She's all grown up with a family all her own. Now, she is MOM. In the beginning, things were confusing. She spent a good bit of time unlearning what she learned, so she could re-learn something new. But she learned. She didn't have a blueprint to follow, so she drafted her own. She had a dream in her heart that was bigger than her past reality, and she was determined to be brave enough to learn how to make it happen. And she did. She rewrote what was written down and handed to her, and she made it her story. Someday, it will be her children's, and they will make it theirs.

I believe there's a Mystery within all of us: beginnings not quite what we expected, dreams deferred, loved ones that have died unexpectedly, or wolves disguised as sheep that have passed through our lives, leaving a trail of pain, sorrow, trauma, abuse, and heartbreak. We all have a story to tell, and we've all encountered experiences that have made us stronger. In Psalms 119:71, the Psalmist said, "For it was good for me that I was afflicted, for if I weren't afflicted I would have never known the power of God."

Life isn't always a mountaintop experience. We want it to be, but it's not. And it shouldn't be. The valleys are where everything grows. We can't live on the mountaintop; the oxygen is so spotty not even the trees can survive up there. Valleys are purposeful. They open our eyes, sharpen our minds, and teach us faith, strength, and patience. The valley provides us with essential mountain-climbing skills that come in many shapes, sizes, and disguises.

The valley is a time of preparation. Mystery suffered a lot of valley experiences before she reached her mountaintop, but it was necessary. The valley gave her strength and endurance for the climb, and now that she's reached the top, nothing can knock her off of it. I encourage you to use Mystery's life as a reference point in understanding that no matter what happens, God is still on the throne. Storms will come, and winds will blow, still, "ALL things work together for the good of them who love God and who are called according to his purpose." (Romans, 8:28).

81955710R00121

Made in the USA
Middletown, DE
30 July 2018